Wild Rose Girls

Shannon Ambroson

Wild Rose Girls

Shannon Ambroson

Published by Shannon Ambroson, 2024.

WILD ROSE GIRLS

First edition. October 4, 2024.

Copyright © 2024 Shannon Ambroson.

ISBN: 979-8227804327

Written by Shannon Ambroson.

Acknowledgments

Thank you to my family and friends, both those who live in the house with me and those scattered around the country. This isn't a story about any of us particularly, but our memories are definitely sprinkled throughout, and I hope you can find them and appreciate how much you mean to me! I absolutely could not have written this without my amazing writing friends in the Tavern Discord and Chaos Chat. Without your guidance and constant support this manuscript would still be just a file on my laptop. We did it, ya'll!

Chapter 1

Sometimes in life there is an event so big, so deep, so traumatic, that a person runs away and never looks back. They never want to think about it again, let alone surround themselves with memories and reminders of the painful time and place.

I called this my Lion King moment; after the big event, I seized the opportunity to run away from my childhood and Hakuna Matata my way through life. I went to college and got straight A's. I met and married a military man after graduation and together we moved all around the country having beautiful adventures together. We had a baby, who grew almost all the way up and is everything we could want–kind, smart, funny, beautiful inside and out, sassy and sarcastic. I absolutely loved my life with my two favorite people in the world, and adored my career as a newspaper journalist. I didn't need to look back; forward was the way to happiness, I was sure of it..

My mind was racing, circling through past and present, as I drove along northbound Interstate 35. With my 17-year-old daughter Lexi beside me on the long trip from San Antonio to small town Iowa, I was a mess of emotions, most of them stemming from the fact that I was just a little older than her when I moved away from Iowa for good. When I'd ran away, I thought to myself bitterly.

"I-35 is the same as ever," I said with a groan, turning my attention back to the present. "It's all road construction and constant traffic!" I glanced at myself in the rear-view mirror, my green eyes bright in the midday sun. I scrunched my face, making crinkly lines appear on the sides. I switched my focus to the road, not wanting to dwell on the wrinkles and fine lines I seemed to notice growing daily.

"But the gas stations are pretty good," Lexi replied, shrugging her shoulders and holding up a giant container of powdered sugared puppy chow and shaking a cup of soda for emphasis. We'd gone from Buccee's to Casey's, stopping any time we needed to stretch, go to the bathroom, or see some weird roadside oddity. Though the businesses along the way changed, the landscape stayed fairly flat with farms and undeveloped land along the busy road.

Lexi and I spent the entire first day just getting out of Texas. We stopped at a roadside hotel in Oklahoma that served Texas shaped waffles for breakfast in the morning, as if every business along the Interstate knew it existed just for drivers to get to and from Texas.

"I love road trips!" Lexi had exclaimed, her mouth full of syrupy waffle. We took so many road trips together over the years and we learned to slow down and just enjoy the little things, like huge waffles and anything that said "world's largest" on the sign. Other than some real traffic outside of Dallas/Fort Worth, this one had gone pretty smoothly.

I glanced over at my daughter, a mess of pink hair and road snacks, lost in her music. I asked myself for the thousandth time if I was doing the wrong thing, taking her out of her school and putting her into a new one a thousand miles away, and for her senior year no less. However, I reminded myself, it didn't seem to matter what life threw at Lexi. She took it and made it work, seeing it as an adventure instead of a bother. It was a trait I knew I passed onto the teen and it made me smile.

She caught my smile and paused her music, looking out at the scenery flying by.

"I don't remember there being so many cornfields," Lexi muttered to herself uncomfortably as she looked out the window of the dirty

SUV. She pulled at her braids, a nervous habit she'd had ever since she was a tot. I nodded, waiting for her to continue.

She sat with her legs crossed over themselves, with her bag of snacks, a pillow, her phone, and everything else we could shove into the footwell of the passenger side. We had packed the rest of the vehicle with suitcases, awkward shopping bags filled with loose objects, and all the belongings they felt they'd need for a year's time away from home.

"It's not that bad," Lexi said, taking a quick snapshot with her phone. "I'll send this to Dad and see what he says."

I smiled again and shifted in my seat, trying to get comfortable after a couple hours without stopping. I really admired the positive energy that seemed to radiate from Lexi, though she always promised she only mirrored what came from me. She shifted in response and returned the smile. I watched her rub a hand over the soft cloth seat, which was cool and comfortable with the AC blasting, unlike the stickiness of her dad's sports car leather seats. Lexi stretched her legs out as much as the seat would allow, and I started feeling jittery at the thought of being close to our destination.

"Mom, you're tapping your fingers again," she told me, pointing at my nervous habit. I stretched my fingers a bit and laughed, apologizing. "It's ok to be nervous. It's been a billion years since you've set foot in your hometown, and we're sort of stuck there for an entire year. It'd be weird if you weren't a little anxious."

She knew me well. When David, my husband and Lexi's dad, left last week, I lost it. I'd cried for hours, and once I'd calmed myself and could speak again, he made me promise to lean on Lexi and my family when I needed it. I just shook it off and told him I'd eventually get to where it felt like any regular move across the country.

To be fair, it sort of was.

At 17, Lexi had lived in 8 states, and I had a couple more on her from life before she was born. Every few years, if we were lucky enough to stay that long, our family packed up and moved to the next base, or the next remote location. I would close up my job at whatever small-town newspaper I worked at and move on, hoping the new town had an opening for full time or freelance at their publication. Lexi would say goodbye to whatever friends she bothered to make to start a new school where she mostly kept quiet and focused on getting through until the next time David would come home with "good news" about his next promotion or his next assignment. It was a routine that we continued over and over, knowing it was all part of the unique life we lived. It wasn't something just everyone understood, that's for sure.

This time his assignment, a 365 deployment, took him across the world where we couldn't follow. David came home early from work one Friday night, sat us down with a less than excited look on his face and told us we would have to stay in Texas without him. He had to leave, and Lexi would go through senior year and possibly graduation without him.

We'd all cried and hugged each other. Lexi had thrown a teenage fit, being extra dramatic on purpose to make us feel guilty. She yelled at us, saying she just wanted one year where her world didn't crash. I listened, I comforted, I told her I completely understood, and then I took a deep breath and immediately began planning.

On the outside I probably hadn't even seemed shocked or upset, though on the inside I was a Texas-sized tornado of emotion. That was me, in a nutshell—tough on the outside, the family's rock, while barely admitting I needed help or support too. Like a duck in a pond, furiously paddling beneath the water while swimming calmly and elegantly above the surface. No one usually bothered to look at how hard I actually worked to make everyone's lives easier, but I continued to do it, regardless. Lexi deserved to feel her emotions, knowing I'd be there to put everything right.

"I was thinking about that night Dad told us he was leaving," Lexi said from the passenger seat, bringing me back to the present. "It was like one thing after another that whole week, remember?"

I nodded, laughing at the mess that week brought. We'd gone through the usual conversations about what to do, how to handle the year apart, when the landlord threw out the last of the bad news: our house was going up for sale and we either needed to buy it or get out.

"Dad has to deploy, ok fine," Lexi continued. "But wait, this time it's for a whole year, oh and we can't go along because it's too dangerous or whatever. And then–MOM AND THEN–the landlord comes at us with an eviction notice?" She threw her hands up and laughed, remembering the shock of it all.

"And THEN," she continued, "you somehow decided that the answer was to move us to the Midwest to stay with grandparents I've barely ever seen, during my last year of high school. Mom, this is nuts. Are you sure we thought this through?"

I took a deep breath, nodded to myself, and forced a smile and told Lexi I sure hoped so. I had made that final decision on my own, as I often needed to do for the family in times of crisis. I'd called my mother and humbled myself real quick.

"Lexi's senior year in the sticks." I said to her, laughing. "You poor dear."

She hit at me, sticking her tongue out.

"It'll be so good for us, love," I went on, reaching over to pat her hand. "We've lived in the city long enough. It's time to lean on family; your Grama and Grampa are so excited to see you before you go away forever for college."

A year sounded like an eternity to us both, though we didn't need to–and wouldn't–say it out loud. We suffered the awkward pause for a moment, each grimacing at the thought. I was the first to break the silence, seeing the road signs begin to change.

"I don't remember THIS many fields..." I said again, snorting a laugh. "It's also more flat than I remember." I grimaced again. "No skyscrapers. No mountains. No beach."

"Just corn," Lexi mumbled with a sigh, sliding down in her seat a bit. She flipped on the phone's bluetooth, letting music blast into her hearing aids.

I knew Lexi needed some vibe shifting before getting to the farm, and frankly so did I, though I kept the car speakers off for her benefit. I also knew we both needed this move, as crazy as it sounded. It was time to go home, to repair the damage I had caused to my family, while there was still time. My Lion King moment didn't end with songs and dancing. It was time to get real. I knew eventually I'd have to explain everything to my daughter, the whole long heartbreaking story.

But right then I just needed to find temporary peace in my choices. It would be nice to show Lexi where I spent my teenage years, before everything happened. It'd been so long since I'd been back on the farm. Would everything feel the same? Would it feel like before?

"So much corn," I mumbled, shaking my head lightly. Honestly though, it was beautiful in its own way. I'd spent a lot of years in those fields. Like my daughter, I was an only child, but my cousins were as close as siblings, closer even. We spent hot sweaty summers together from sunup to sundown, mostly running around outside away from the eyes and ears of our parents, who would throw a chore or two at us if they saw us. As much as I wanted to forget it, those fields and those people made me who I am. They're a part of me–a part of Lexi.

I took a deep breath as I passed the county line.

Ready or not. Jenna Rose Abbott was Home.

Chapter 2

We weren't even fully into the driveway when my mother, the one and only Dottie Rose, came shuffling out to greet us. She looked so far removed from the poor farmer's wife I left 20 years ago, with her pressed white collared shirt and pressed Levi's jeans, her platform espadrilles moving heavily over the gravel. She wore a silk scarf around her neck and gold bracelets jangled on her wrist as she opened Lexi's door and practically dragged her out to greet her.

"Alexis, I am just SO happy you're here!" Dottie said enthusiastically. She hugged my awkward teen, her arms folding all the way around Lexi's thin body. I watched her fingers clasp around the back of my daughter. Fingers laced with wrinkles and soft pink paint on carefully manicured nails. It'd been so long since I'd see my mother, and I cleared my throat, pushing the emotion away as she pulled her arms back and looked between the two of us, her own eyes watery.

"We cleaned up the rooms in the back," she said to us before reaching out to rub Lexi's arms in that motherly way she used to do to me. "I thought maybe you could stay out there while your mom takes the guest room upstairs. You might like your privacy, you know," she rambled. "I remember your mom at that age, always loving to be on her own. Did she tell you about the old playhouse?"

Lexi shook her head and snuck a look to me, wide eyed. It was the look of panic and I smirked and snorted.

"Mom, we talked about this. I haven't mentioned much of anything to Lexi and that's ok. We can both bunk in the guest room in your house. I was thinking once a rental comes up we can get out of your hair altogether. Small towns aren't exactly thriving in the housing market right now."

Dottie started rambling again about knowing a perfect realtor and then stopped to tell me we would do no such thing. There was plenty of room at the farm, she told me again, and we would not embarrass her by staying in some bed-and-breakfast all year.

I nodded and turned to look at the place I'd left all those years ago; it'd been a couple decades since I'd set foot on this property.

The large farmhouse wasn't much to look at, but it was classic and modest with its two stories and wrap-around porch, all painted stark white. Dottie had decorated the front in red, white, and blue for the summer Americana holidays. They kept the siding clean and the windows spotless. The home looked both loved and lived in but also looked too big for her parents to keep up on their own. I knew my mom had called in many favors to help the old place look its best. She dealt in batches of cookies and Sunday roasts, if things hadn't changed.

I slipped my arm through Lexi's, guiding her away from my mom for a minute. I noticed my dad wasn't anywhere near, which meant he was either working on something or just didn't want to see me yet. I was equal parts angry and thankful.

We walked along the garden blocks back behind the house toward the "playhouse" I used to spend so much time in as a kid. Seeing it as a full-grown adult I of course realized it wasn't a playhouse at all, but a small house in its own right. I smiled to myself as Lexi's eyes went wide and she flew out of my reach. In Texas she and her friends had been obsessed with a television show that would flip tiny homes into dream homes, and I could tell she was dying to get a photo on her phone to send to them. She'd have her phone out before I could catch up to her.

The small house was plain, clean, and looked as though someone had recently worked on it. Short, simple roofline, windows with shutters, and planter boxes in the front, the place was a grown-up version of what I remembered.

"It's beautiful, Mom," I said, letting out a breath. Lexi nodded, biting her lip in excitement. She slipped her phone into her pocket and looked to Dottie as she continued her rambling.

"Way back this place used to house the seasonal farmhands that came throughout the year to help with the planting and harvest," Dottie explained to Lexi. "This farm has been in our family for generations and we're real proud of the way your ancestors took care of their workers, who sometimes came in from out of town, working all those long hours." She shook her head in wonderment before swatting away a fly and continuing. "The poor house sat empty for a while until we turned it into a playhouse for your mama when she was young. We thought maybe you'd use it too, but you never visited..." Dottie caught her sour face and smiled meekly.

"Everyone said to turn it into one of those short-term rental types, but I just don't want strangers here all the time. We turned it into a guest house but it's mostly just sat there empty waiting for someone to come in and make it her own." She winked at Lexi. "We fixed it up a little but I'm sure there's still a lot that a teenage girl could do with a summer and a small budget."

I stared at the pair, my brow furrowed, wondering how long to let the two of them scheme about decorating. I opened and closed my mouth twice and waited while they talked about color palettes and fabrics. Lexi was beaming.

Finally, I needed to set the boundary. I just couldn't take it any longer.

"Mom, you know Lexi can't stay out here alone," I started gently. "She and I can stay back here together. I'll hold off looking at rentals right now since there aren't any anyway, and we'll just see how we do. I don't want us to be in your way at all."

My teen shot me a look. In the past few minutes, she'd probably gotten used to the idea of having the space to herself.

"Final," I said to her, raising my brow. She shrugged and looked around behind the house. I saw her frown and shudder a bit, which caused me to let out, a laugh. I knew what she was thinking before she could say anything.

"Grama Dottie, are there ever animals living in this corn?" Lexi asked weakly, still grimacing a bit.

Dottie let out a hearty laugh, stopping short when she met Lexi's serious eyes.

"Your mom hasn't been filling your head with stories has she?" She sent me a look, and I put my hands up and shook my head. My mother didn't even glance my way as she kept talking.

"You know, if she hadn't been sneaking out that night she wouldn't have ever stepped on that snake anyhow." Lexi's jaw dropped as she looked from me to my mother. I schooled my face, enjoying the interaction way too much. "Now, let's see about airing out this place and making sure you have everything you need. We'll have dinner in the main house at 5:30 and lunch after church on Sunday. Of course you're welcome to join us for breakfast anytime. We're always here, unless I'm with my card club or quilting or shopping, or doing chores..."

I put a hand gently on my mom's arm. She was nervous; it was obvious. I didn't want her to scare Lexi off before we even unpacked. I changed the subject, asking mom about the land and who owned it now. I needed her to talk about something that would calm her back down, whether I actually cared or knew who the neighbors even were at that point.

Lexi winked and mouthed a thank you, tiptoeing to the door to the guest cottage. I motioned for her to go on in while I kept Dottie talking for a few minutes. I figured it was only fair to give my kid a chance to look around on her own before we attempted to cram into the small house with my mother's large personality.

Holding the door for Dottie, I waited for her to go in behind Lexi, following her through the surprisingly heavy wooden door. I let the screen door slam closed, making a note to catch it next time. It felt so cozy as we walked inside the tiny entryway. Immediately my mind swirled with memories of the sounds, the smells, the constant children running around. I stood there letting the memories tornado around me feeling frozen in time.

Lexi called to me, breaking me out of my quiet panic. She held up a white stoneware bowl that said "Keys" on it, telling me how cute it was sitting on a small table in the entryway. I looked around with fresh eyes, noticing the small coat closet, the hardwood flooring, the gray walls with white trim. I looked to the small but open kitchen to the right, which looked like Dottie and Charles had updated it at some point. I followed along to the circular dining table and four chairs, the small living space to the left, with a couch and two dark leather rockers, and a hallway with 3 doors. Two cramped bedrooms with a small bathroom between them.

"One bathroom?" Lexi asked, shocked. I smiled, remembering sitting on a stool in that bathroom getting my hair done or applying makeup with my cousins.

Dottie had decorated everything in that modern farmhouse design, with gray and white colors throughout. Lexi chose the first bedroom, throwing her bag on the quilted bed. No doubt Dottie had quilted it herself, I thought.

The whole space was smaller than our apartment in Georgia, where we had learned to walk up 3 flights of stairs with bags of groceries we'd bought from the corner market. We'd shared a cluttered bathroom then too, but we'd found our way.

We'd do the same here.

Lexi jumped in front of me, a smile crawling across her face.

"Mom, it's so cute! Should we unload now?"

I nodded as we propped open the door for a bunch of trips in and out. We'd packed as light as we could, since everything had to fit in the SUV. It had been difficult deciding which items to choose, but somehow we made it work. All the household furniture and whatever we couldn't fit into the car went into storage to deal with later when the deployment is over, when we move back to San Antonio.

If we move back to San Antonio, I thought, my heart aching for the life we left. We hadn't talked much about that part. We hadn't asked Lexi what she thought about any of it. We just hadn't had a chance; David had to be ready to ship out, and we had a checklist to follow to not a lot of time to do it. We put everything else on hold, including Lexi's ACT and SAT tests, her college and scholarship applications, and anything related to the future beyond the deployment.

Shoving the guilt back to revisit later, I thanked my mother again and told her the house was beautiful. She smiled modestly but stood a little taller with the compliment.

"Your dad went to a lot of trouble to fix this place up, though he'll never admit it," Dottie told us. My father was a quiet, proud man who hated fuss and liked to get things done quickly and efficiently. I had a hard time imagining him caring enough to put thought into decisions based on what I might like. Probably he just enjoyed the projects and preferred Dottie direct him what to do.

"Well, we will definitely thank him when we see him," I told her, looking at Lexi with a nod. To her I said, "Yes, Lex, let's get a bit of unpacking done before dinner. Tomorrow we can look around a bit and figure out how to get you enrolled at school."

Lexi groaned, as if she'd forgotten all about her senior year starting in just a few months. She looked out through the window at the growing cornstalks. I briefly wondered how tall they'd get and when they'd get cut down. I couldn't even remember, but I knew the landscape would look so different without them.

School here wouldn't be that much different from Texas, would it? Or any of the other states we'd lived in? I was glad we had the summer to settle in before starting it all again. My thoughts raced again as we began unloading the car, humidity blasting every time we stepped outside.

Fresh start, I said to myself over and over. Fresh start. Right.

I missed David.

Chapter 3

1993

As a child I loved summers more than any time of year—more than Christmas or Halloween or that time in the spring where it got warm before the last winter chill. Summers on the farm were lazy, simple, and always super special to my entire family. The days were long, and the weeks were short. Popsicles, cans of soda, watermelon and sweet corn for dinner—I loved it all and wished it would last all year.

As an only child, nights during the school year meant homework and playing alone while my parents finished chores or played cards with the neighbors. I spent weekends together with my aunts and cousins when we could all find time, but it seemed like the grownups were always busy. I spent most of my time alone writing stories to read to my stuffed animals.

But summers in small town Willow, Iowa, were magical. May 1993, I turned 10 on the last day of school, and I sprinted outside when the bell rang, my heavy backpack overflowing with broken crayons and notebooks filled with doodles and drawings of cats.

"Mommy, I'm ready!" I called into the window of my mother's brown station wagon. "I'm ready for my birthday!"

My mother Dottie clapped and told me to hurry and get in. She had a huge surprise for me and couldn't wait to show it off. I awkwardly climbed inside the large vehicle, setting my backpack at my feet and placing them gently on top of it, my knees knocking together with joyfulness. I struggled with my seatbelt and gave an exasperated puff of air and a thumbs up when I finished, hugging my legs to pull all the excitement into my body.

Dottie didn't smoke in our car like some of my friends' moms did. I inhaled the smell of pine from the little air freshener shaped like a Christmas tree that hung from the rear-view mirror. Dottie kept the car clean, and I enjoyed running my hands along the smooth cloth seats that to my little hands felt like expensive velvet.

We drove back to our cozy white farmhouse singing songs from the radio. Janet Jackson was my favorite that year, and I really wanted a cassette player and Janet Jackson tape wrapped in pretty paper and a bow for my birthday. I'd dropped hints for months so I just knew someone would get it for me.

"OK, Jenna, close your eyes!" Dottie told me after we parked the car and dropped my backpack on the porch. "Follow along with me. There you go, just around here. I've got you," Dottie led me slowly around to the backyard toward the fields. "Now OPEN THEM!"

I slowly opened one eye, then the other, and smirked. All I saw was the old farmwork house, and I scrunched up my face in confusion.

"Mommy, what's so special about the weird old house?" I asked. Dottie motioned toward the house, which on second glance looked freshly painted and cleaner than I'd last seen it. Did someone move in?

"Go inside and see!"

A smile spread across my wide face and I brushed my hands down my new denim dress, ready for a birthday adventure. I rushed to open the door, immediately greeted with shouts of Happy Birthday from almost everyone I knew—everyone important to me. I couldn't think of another time I'd been so happy and surprised.

My dad Charles held a beautiful pink cake with icing flowers and my name written on top in pretty cursive letters. J-E-N-N-A. Beside him my twin cousins Tina and Tyler stood next to their mom, my aunt Bloom. The twins poked at each other to scoot over while their mom whispered to them with an impatient look on her face. I noticed my aunt Rebecka keeping my older cousin Lauren's hands out of the ice cream, giggles and squeals erupting from them both.

I felt so loved and content whenever my family was around, but a birthday party on the last day of school felt like just about the most special thing in the entire world.

A quick knock sounded, and the door opened again behind me. I found myself instantly surrounded in a hug from my best friend Penny.

"I knew about this the whoooollleeee time!" Penny giggled to me. "I kept a secret! We made a party for you and you didn't even know!" We'd gone the whole day at school and the secret never came out. I nodded at my friend, impressed.

"Penny, how did you keep it a secret the WHOLE DAY?" I squealed to my friend. "We were together all the time and you can never keep secrets!" Penny rolled her eyes and grumbled that she could so keep secrets, but then saw the cake and gasped loudly, pointing out the flowers made from frosting.

I looked up at my mom with the best idea my 10-year-old brain could imagine.

"I don't know who lives here, but I'm going to name this house Wild Rose House, because we're wild like flowers and they're about the prettiest thing ever! AND we're the Roses, right Mommy?" I looked at the flowers on my cake and stuck a finger in one, bringing the sugary buttercream to my mouth as Dottie swatted my small hand away lovingly.

"I guess that makes YOU the Wild Rose Girls," Dottie laughed. Ty called out, "And boy!" and everyone joined in the laughter. He didn't know why we laughed, but he loved the attention.

Dottie scooted us girls toward the cake and told me to make a wish and blow out the candles. I wished again for my cassette player and for my cousins and friend to always be here with me forever and always.

Chapter 4

"Hey peanut, how's Iowa?" I heard David ask over the video chat. Lexi called him once we finished unpacking the SUV to check that the house does in fact have normal working internet. David was dressed in his military issued flight suit and I could see he'd already started growing his deployment mustache.

"Did Dottie stuff you into some overalls and make you walk the fields yet?" he asked her with a smile. I tried to leave them to their conversation but couldn't help but just stand outside the door for a few minutes. I missed having the three of us in the same room. In the same time zone.

"Dad, who can think about overalls right now with that thing on your face?" she teased him. Lexi and I always hated the deployment 'stache. It was a tradition for him to grow it, just as it was a tradition for Lexi to help him shave it when he returned.

It was the middle of the night for him, but he always answered when Lexi called—whenever he could, anyway. As soon as he answered she immediately started babbling about animals in the fields, telling him what she'd learned from a quick Google search.

He laughed at his daughter's joke and must have made a face, because she giggled and told him to stop or his face would stay frozen that way. As always, video chatting would get harder once he got acclimated to the new time zone and started flying his missions. Everyone was happy to have a little face time before the impending radio silence.

"And no, no overalls! It's not happening, even if Fashion Flare Magazine declares them the trend of the year!" she laughed. "Grama's got this little house in the backyard and she's fixed it all up for us, so we have our own rooms and a kitchen and all that. I can't believe Mom's never mentioned it before."

I cringed, knowing there was so much I hadn't ever mentioned.

"Mom calls it Wild Rose House," she went on, "which is pretty cute, actually. Do you think Mom was wild as a kid?"

David yawned, the jetlag catching up to him. Flying over the ocean in the back of a cargo plane was a far cry from the first-class seats we always splurged on when we took our annual summer vacations.

"Not as wild as you will be this summer, I bet. I can't wait to hear how you settle in! I hope you'll take this one seriously and try to plant your roots, yeah?"

Lexi groaned, and I laughed to myself. I'd told her almost exactly the same thing on the drive.

"It's going to be a shallow planting, Dad..." Lexi started. I heard a soft sigh in understanding, and then silence while he waited for a real answer. "Yes, I'll try," Lexi finished. I heard a smile in her voice. I loved that girl so much.

"Sweetheart, I need to go now. I have to get a couple hours sleep before we head out, alright? Write everything down and email it to me, like always. It helps us both."

Lexi promised she would, her voice cracking. She knew communication from then on would be difficult, and they'd start in with the next tradition: daily journal writings. She started journaling when she was first able to type; she must have been about 8 years old, and it took her forever to finish writing each entry. It was a few sentences a day, letting her father know who she played with at recess or what they had for lunch. Lexi would ask me to proofread it for her like I would if it was a newspaper article, and my heart swelled every time she'd trust me with the words meant for her dad. David deployed so many times over the years, but usually just for a few months, so those journal entries quickly became countdowns to homecomings.

This time it would be so many months, and I couldn't imagine Lexi writing every day, filling up space with life in the cornfields and church socials. But she promised she'd try, and I knew she would.

"Goodnight Dad," Lexi told him. I peeked further around the corner to see her moving her fingers into the sign for "I love you" and smiling when he returned the gesture. "Good luck, stay safe, go get em, and all that."

They hung up, and I went to my room. I sat on the quilted bed and cried, big fat tears, knowing Lexi probably did the same thing in her room. I cried until I felt dehydrated and weak. Taking a deep breath, I promised myself I'd also give this place an actual try. I agreed with Lexi though–no overalls.

Chapter 5

I had always worked, ever since I was 16 years old. I was so sad to quit my job in San Antonio, an editor for the Express-News, when we'd decided to move across the country again. It had been a while since I'd been a field reporter, working problematic hours to get the story. As I walked into the Willow newspaper office, I remembered the years of chasing news stories and following firetrucks. I hadn't wanted to get back into it this way, but when I found out the newspaper was about to fold as I was moving back into town, it just seemed destined. I couldn't just let the paper fail if they'd be willing to let me try to save it.

"Hello, Mr. Smith, I'm here to get started!" I greeted the Editor-in-Chief, an aged gentleman wearing a bow tie and oversized thick glasses. "How can I help?"

The gray-haired publisher, who I'd known since I was a kid, sighed in relief at the sight of me. He pulled me in for a handshake, grasping my hand with both of his, taking me by surprise.

"I am so glad you're here!" he assured me, apologizing for being so emotional. "It's been a bit of a mess around here for way too long. I really thought we were going to lose it. I hope there's enough here to save."

He showed me around the messy workspace. The building was expansive and felt empty, our voices echoing through the high ceilings. I looked around at the exposed ductwork and beams, and at the empty cubicles. No other employees sat at the heavy wooden desks. Other than a couple temporary volunteers, Mr. Smith was the last remaining staff member.

I closed my eyes for a moment and imagined a full staff bustling around a thriving office. I vowed to make that a reality, somehow. If there was one thing I enjoyed, it was a work challenge. I pulled a notepad from my bag and started taking notes as Mr. Smith showed me around and talked to me about how things used to work before the breakdown.

I spent the rest of the day getting to know the office, learning that every single bit of tech and software was at least a decade behind, and taking deep breaths in a constant state of overwhelm bordering on panic. I was filling the notepad with my careful scrawls but I formed strategies as I wrote, and my hope was bigger than my fear.

The news staff had all retired or moved onto bigger outlets, and there was no one to fill in anywhere. My job was to figure out how to find new staff, upgrade outdated equipment and software, and organize the office, all with almost no budget, and in the meantime do what I could to print a paper once a week. I sighed and reminded myself I'd seen worse.

At one time the Willow Gazette printed daily issues, and distributed them among multiple small towns as the go-to for news and features south of Des Moines. Like everything printed, it slowly withered away to a smaller, less frequent distribution, unable to compete with the state capital's online and social media driven instant news. People looked to bloggers and influencers to tell them what was happening in the world. Small town news just didn't sell enough to break a profit.

"I wonder if I can pay Lexi to help me do those reels," I mumbled to myself, looking at my notes again. I laughed at the thought of me dancing and reading news stories on the internet. We'd get views alright, snorting out loud. I crossed out that idea, knowing full well I'd embarrass myself more than I'd gather support for the cause.

I'd found my way through years of moving by freelancing or temping at every newspaper I could. I took literally any news job—or news adjacent job–that would hire me. My resume was a mess, but I knew my way around the industry and my references were impeccable.

Reviving the paper would be tricky but I just needed the right people beside me to get it back on track. It was hard to find specifically educated people in a small town, or people willing to move to a small town for a job that paid next to nothing, but hard didn't mean impossible. I was no stranger to hard.

I knew from experience that you didn't need a degree to write. It helped, but talent and drive was more important. I'd had plenty of employees without degrees prove their worth time after time with their words. My first thought was my old friend Penny, who I hadn't spoken with in decades. I brushed it aside. We'd both loved writing when we were in high school, and I remembered Penny having a real knack for it, but that was so many years ago. We hadn't spoken since graduation and honestly after all these years it embarrassed me to be so out of touch with someone who was in my life every day as a kid. I wasn't sure where Penny lived anymore, or what her life was like. Maybe she'd moved away to find fame after high school. Or maybe she still worked around town somewhere.

No, there would need to be a job posting and applications, interviews and hiring trials. I'd do this the right way. The long way, I thought with a groan.

I sat down at the computer and drafted a job post.

"I might as well get started," I mumbled aloud to myself. It would probably be a long and boring and potentially lonely day, with Mr. Smith coming and going as he inched closer and closer to being done for good. The quicker I got the word out and hired someone the quicker I'd have someone at work to call a friend, and the less overwhelming the whole newspaper process would become. No one could do it alone.

"And then maybe I can stop mumbling to myself," I said to no one, sighing.

Chapter 6

I got home from work Monday afternoon, groceries in hand, to see Lexi typing away on her computer. Seeing me coming in, she placed her laptop on the counter and rushed to help me unload the rest of the grocery bags from the car.

"Thank you, there's literally nothing in this house to eat!" she told me dramatically. I nodded, thinking about the protein bar I'd dug through my purse to find before work. I'd been so excited to find it and had scarfed it down before guiltily realizing Lexi would have nothing to eat. I'd left her a note and some cash to go to the cafe downtown. It was the best I could do, promising I'd get actual food on the way home.

Now I was exhausted, but it felt good to get the house in order a bit. I gave Lexi a quick hug, and we finished putting everything away together. I motioned to her laptop and asked if she'd finished her email. She nodded and asked if I'd proof it for her.

"I'm working on my descriptive writing," she told me. I was a little too excited about her taking an interest in writing and to find out what she'd done while I was at work, but I calmly nodded back and sat down at the table to read her letter to David.

Dear Dad,

After a couple days of unpacking and sulking, I got up this morning with purpose. I wove my long pink hair into a dutch braid, laced up my pink Converse shoes, and went into the kitchen searching for breakfast. (PS how's that for imagery? Mom's helping me work on my writing)

Mom had left for work and the fridge was still empty, as neither of us had yet to venture to the store, and apparently grocery delivery isn't a thing in a small midwestern town. I really didn't want to go into the main house and get stuck listening to Grama Dottie go on and on again about my hair color choice, or worse yet invite me to join her at the church for whatever crafty old lady group was in session that day.

Mom left a note and some money and told me to find the coffee shop downtown. It's walkable, she said. It isn't fair for a 17-year-old to live without a car, but that's a whole 'nother thing I guess. We'll argue that cruel and unusual punishment another day. For today, I laced up my Chucks and got to walking. She was right, of course, downtown wasn't too far away.

It's pretty cute around here, in a weird back-in-time sort of way, with green grass, wildflowers along the road, and those little paint-chipped picket fences that look as though they belong in a movie. I even heard birds chirping and dogs barking, which you know is tough for me to do with my hearing aids. I guess we'd gotten so used to cars and buses and constant honking and construction drowning everything out in the city!

So apparently there's one spot to get coffee here, unless you want to go to the gas station. On my way I also noticed a bar, a fabric shop, one of those catch-all mercantile stores, a couple restaurants, a large bank, a dance studio with tutus and streamers in the window, and finally, the coffee shop, with its chalkboard sign and constant stream of people heading in and out of the heavy glass door.

It was busier than the rest of the shops, and for a minute I almost felt like I was back in San Antonio. Fewer cowboy hats, leather boots and purses, and more denim, baseball hats, and canvas tote bags. Someone tacked Willow High sports posters and musical tryout ads in the windows. Mom told me once that Texas was just like Iowa but with spurs and professional sports teams, and after this morning I immediately understood the comparison.

Anyway, you know coffee is my favorite smell in the entire world, and coffee shops and bookstores are my happy places. I will take an oversized chair with a warm mug in my hands over almost anything else. Cafes are a portal to a place of certainty and sameness, and I can always count on them no matter where we live. (Mom really likes that line)

The lady at the counter freaked out when she saw me.

"You look just like your mama," she told me. "Except for the hair." She said she heard Mom was back in town and that they hadn't spoken in years. She seemed nervous though, sort of anxious.

I asked her if she knew Mom in high school or something and she said they graduated together. Penny or something. She was NOT shy about keeping inside her personal space bubble. I really just wanted my coffee, but I promise I was nice.

Let me see if I can describe the cafe for you. It smelled like that perfect mix of sugar and bitter coffee. It was larger than it looked from the outside, with a handful of tables in the center for breakfast groups, chairs and couches set up along the window, and a smaller room off the main dining area with overflow seating. Everything was cozy and worn in, with acoustic music playing quietly. I chose a brown leather chair in the corner where I could spy on everyone coming in and out.

I set my coffee and muffin on a table, beside a stack of magazines, a couple romance novels, the latest crime mystery from an author that Mom sometimes reads, and a worn copy of last week's Willow Gazette.

The muffin was top-notch, and the coffee was just as good as anywhere in the city. I decided to people-watch for a bit like we always do when we're together.

There were more than a few moms with babies in their arms, trying to juggle diaper bags and their sugary lattes, searching for loose change to add to the tip jar. There were business suits stirring creamer into their large coffees to go. There were groups of people meeting for a quick breakfast before lazing around on their precious summer day, not that different from any other cafe. It was comforting, and so charming to watch everyone greet each other kindly and thank each other for everything. People even hugged when they ran into a friendly face and made plans to see each other at some event or another coming up in the future. Everyone reminded me of Mom.

Then I met a girl who works at the coffee shop who is about my age. This is so weird, are you ready? She has hearing aids just like me. Her hair is blond, and she had it pulled up into a high ponytail, so I noticed them immediately. When I pointed out mine to her, she literally yelled "no way!" and stopped to talk to me. I know I rolled my eyes when you told me I'd probably meet my new best friend immediately, but I'll admit, you might be right.

Her name is Sophie. We laughed a lot, and I gave her my phone number so she can text me about school. She had to get back to work, so I sat there and watched people some more. I read through the newspaper Mom's going to supposedly save, and oh boy, I think she has a lot of work to do.

Anyway, I hope you're doing well! Until next time,

Lexi

"Lexi, your writing is fabulous! Do you want a job at the paper?" I asked her, helping her fix a few typos and urging her to go ahead and send it. She rolled her eyes and said the one email took her more than an hour to get just right.

"You can't afford me," she said, winking. "Maybe someday."

We laughed and planned dinner. It'd been a while since we'd cooked together, just the two of us, and we fell back into our routine pretty quickly. I bit my tongue, wanting to ask about Penny, but not wanting to offer anything more than absolutely necessary. It was such a small town thing for Lexi to run into Penny when I'd just been wondering about her. Instead of grilling her for information, I listened to her tell me about her walk home and the kitten she tried to befriend, and how adorable she found the neighborhoods in Willow. I couldn't think of a way to bring up the conversation without offering information about my past, which I just wasn't ready to discuss.

Sometimes being a parent and a woman with a whole life before becoming that parent is just difficult to navigate. I was going to need to find that balance quickly and calmly so I could stay ahead of myself.

How quickly did old news travel in a small town?

Chapter 7

1994

I loved having a birthday that fell between school ending and summer beginning. I had time to plan a party during those last few days of monotonous end-of-the-year tests and teacher monologues. Every year the party would come to symbolize the beginning of summer, a kickoff for Wild Rose House.

Dottie was the first to call us the Wild Rose Girls, and I loved the name. It made me feel special, like we had her own special club that no one else could join. My friend Penny and I, along with my cousins Lauren and Tina, were always playing in the "playhouse" I had named Wild Rose House. Tina's twin, Tyler, would hang out sometimes, but would often bow out of the more "girlie" activities and go play with his own friends away from what he called was cootie central.

I wanted to go camping on my 11th birthday. It was warm enough but Dottie didn't trust us outside so close to the fields so she made a compromise with us kids. We could put sleeping bags on the playhouse floor and Dottie would sleep in the bedroom, nearby but giving us a bit of privacy for our preteen fun.

Tyler joined us girls that time, because cake and ghost stories were more important than anything else he could think of at 11 years old. He and Tina hadn't gotten to have a party when they'd turned 11 a few months ago, so I promised they could pretend we were triplets sharing a party together.

"I brought you the best gift ever," Penny told me as we sat at the table, cake in between us. "You should open mine first!"

Lauren, who had turned 12 on her last birthday, rolled her eyes.

"You can't just assume yours is the best, Penny," she complained, scrunching her face in annoyance. "Mine's pretty good too, and I'm older so I know what to get more than you do."

Lauren always slighted Penny, reminding her she wasn't a cousin. "You're not a real Wild Rose Girl" she'd tell her. "Not like me, Jenna, and Tina." Penny would always cry and run off, leaving me to huff at my cousin and go calm my friend down.

"I'll love them both," I said, trying to smooth things over. "I'll just close my eyes and pick so I don't know which is which, ok?"

Lauren had given me an Ace of Base cassette tape. I had gotten my Sony Walkman on my last birthday just as I'd wished. My eyes lit up as I tore the wrapping paper off. I squealed and told my cousin thank you with a big hug.

"We can go listen now!" Lauren exclaimed.

"NO!" yelled Penny. "She hasn't opened my gift yet, Lauren!" The girls stuck their tongues out at each other and I had to tell them again to be nice to each other.

Tina and Ty just sat and watched the whole thing, embarrassed that they hadn't brought gifts. Tina had drawn a homemade card for me and Tyler had signed his name to the bottom alongside his sister.

I smiled at everyone and told them it's all ok. "I'll open Penny's present and then we can listen to Ace of Base on my mom's boom box while we eat cake!" I'd always had a way of making everyone in the room feel at ease. It was my superpower I guess, and my cousins were better for it.

Penny handed me a box with gold wrapping paper. She'd put cat and dog stickers all over the outside so I would know it was special. I had a hard time opening the paper, trying not to rip any of the stickers.

"It's a BFF necklace!" Penny announced as I carefully pulled the lid from the box, barely seeing what was inside. "Look, I already have the other half!" she exclaimed as she pulled a heart-shaped necklace from beneath her shirt.

"I hid it from you all day! I'm so good at keeping surprises from you, Jenna. Now we can always remember each other when we aren't together," she said.

I thanked Penny and put the necklace around my neck. Tyler had already gotten into the cake and Tina was hitting at his frosting covered hand, yelling at him to stop ruining everything.

"I love it, thank you," I said, tears forming in my eyes. "I love all of you, even you Tyler, who can't seem to WAIT to eat the birthday girl's CAKE." I glared at him sharply.

"You said it was our birthday party too," Tyler mumbled, but then laughed as he raised his hand. He jumped up and put his frosting fingers in front of him, claiming to be the cake monster, chasing us all around the room as we squealed and screamed.

Then we all took fistfuls of cake and ran around being cake monsters. That was Ty's special talent, his superpower, being able to make any room fun. Everyone was a cake monster. Everyone was a Wild Rose Girl.

Chapter 8

I needed coffee. I was off to my 3rd full day of work, but felt like my hundredth. There was so much that needed to be done to hire a staff, and actively publish a newspaper on top of it. The budget was next to nothing, there was no ad sales department currently, and Mr. Smith was one foot out the door, already talking about plans to retire on a beach somewhere.

"Margaritas and sunshine," he kept saying. "After a life landlocked, I'm gonna find me some ocean!" Midwestern people were often obsessed with the ocean, like it was the stuff of legends. When I was a kid, it seemed everyone around me wanted to be a marine biologist, and the parents laughed and asked which lake they're going to study, as if no one ever leaves Iowa. To be honest, most of the people in this town had been born there, so I guess they weren't too far off.

Caffeine, I reminded myself. To battle my Wednesday morning headache, I needed the good stuff. Lexi and I usually made coffee at home, always making enough for the both of us before we left for work or school. But I didn't know where the coffeemaker was, or if we even still had one with the rush of putting most of our things in storage. Lexi must have been getting her caffeine somewhere though, the cafe downtown maybe. That girl is as addicted to coffee as her mother, I thought with a smirk.

That morning I needed an oat milk latte, and I knew there was only one place in town to get it. The Cup had been there forever, since I could remember. It was Willow's only coffee shop, unless you counted the gas station, and I could practically smell the coffee aroma just thinking about it. I thought about Lexi's email to David and cringed as I thought about who I might run into, but there just wasn't another option, so I had to chance it.

Walking into The Cup was like walking into 1999. It took me back to a time where I worked behind the little counter, brewing and steaming, crafting lattes and cappuccinos the summer I turned 16. I took a deep inhale and closed my eyes a second, thinking back to being that punk kid. I smiled and opened my eyes, panicking as I made eye contact with the worker behind the counter.

"Oh my GAWD, Jenna, I KNEW you'd come in, I just KNEW it! You have always loved a good coffee and you could never stay away from this place. I am so glad to see you!"

Penny.

Penny was here. Working at the cafe. My risk had failed, and now I was face to face with my former best friend. But even knowing she'd probably be there, I couldn't help wonder why was Penny working at the cafe? And why did she look like she wanted to jump over the counter to hug me?

I recovered my panic and smiled cautiously.

"Hi Penny," I said, calmly. "I didn't know you worked here." Lie.

I looked around to see customers struggle to appear as if they weren't watching my every move. Most wouldn't know who I am, but the gossip flows steadily in a small town and they'd figure it out quickly if I gave them the chance.

Penny popped a hand on her hip and smirked. She had piled her brown hair high on her head and she was as pretty as she'd been in high school, even with no makeup on and little lines forming at the corners of her brown eyes.

"You mean your daughter didn't tell you she saw me? She comes in here every day now, and she said nothing?" She clicked her tongue. "Well, I suppose that can't be helped. But YES, I work here. Have for years. But how would you know that? You haven't been here in—"

She stopped talking when she noticed the line of people in the queue and all the eyes looking at our exchange, just waiting for some firsthand gossip to share later. She drew in a breath and gave that Midwestern smile.

"Anyway. What can I get for you dear?"

I smiled back and politely ordered my latte—oat milk and brown sugar, extra hot. I could feel Penny's eyes linger on me as we waited for the barista, a girl with beautiful green eyes that reminded me of Lexi's, to finish making my drink. I took the coffee and thanked the teen–possibly the Sophie I'd heard about–trying not to run into the line of customers. I left quickly, almost tripping on the way out.

Once I was safely down the street a bit, I ducked into an alley to catch my breath, gripping my hot coffee until I felt my hands warm uncomfortably. I'd known I'd run into my old acquaintances, eventually. I'd gone over it in my head what I would do or how I would act.

And yet the moment I saw Penny–who I'd called my best friend for so long–I panicked. I wasn't ready. Thoughts ran through my head like a traffic jam. I shouldn't have come back to Iowa. I should have prepared better. I should have asked my mother where all my former friends and family existed so I'd be ready when they barreled toward me.

I gave myself a couple minutes to collect myself and shook the feelings away. I headed into work with a new confidence to accomplish everything on my to-do list. There would always be people and situations I couldn't control, but work was something I could throw myself into and disassociate from the rest for a bit.

"I haven't even had my caffeine yet," I mumbled the reminder to myself. "I'm just frazzled because my brain's exhausted. I'll feel better soon."

Lie.

Chapter 9

1995

"Pose, Lauren!" I told my cousin, snapping a photo as Lauren blew a kiss to the camera, her light blond curls flowing softly over her shoulders.

I had gotten a new camera for my 12th birthday and I wanted to take pictures of everything so I wouldn't forget a single moment of summer. I loved everything about my life and it all felt important, necessary to chronicle; a time capsule to be unearthed later when we were all older and working fancy important jobs. Maybe I'd make a scrapbook, or beautiful photo albums for all the Wild Rose Girls (and Boy). I would surely be a photographer someday and get paid to take glamorous and mysterious photos of celebrities. TLC and Mariah Carey would beg me to work with them.

"Take my photo, Jenna!" Penny said with all the excitement one would expect from her. I nodded and waited for Penny to pose. She made a kiss face, and held up a peace sign, and immediately after I clicked the button she called out, "And another!"

All of us girls were all hanging out in Wild Rose House, listening to music and dancing around the living room. The kitchen was a mess of cookie dough and chocolate chips. Dottie trusted us girls to bake cookies on our own as long as we promised not to burn down the place. My parents had upgraded the kitchen a bit the previous winter to make it safer now that the small house was being used more often. Dottie loved to show it off and was proud to tell her friends of all the treats her daughter learned to make with her friends.

Penny and I still got along great, but if I was honest, I sometimes wondered if we would have become friends if we'd met at 12 years old instead of when we were toddlers. Penny was loud and excited and bounced around as if she couldn't control her level of love for the world. I was quieter, preferring to read and write, and now take photos from behind the camera. I always preferred to be behind the scenes rather than in front and center.

But we were friends because we'd always been friends. She was family. And the Cousins liked her enough too, so we kept asking her to come to all our parties. I felt Penny would have continued to show up even if we stopped inviting her, honestly. We had woven her into our lives and nothing could untangle her.

Penny was an only child too, and didn't have the best family life. Her parents divorced when she was young and it was just her mom and her in a rundown apartment near the square. Penny hated her own cramped home, which she said smelled like stale air and cigarettes. She wished she could live with me. She wanted to BE me. She'd told me many times, and it always made me feel a little guilty and uncomfortable.

Lauren and Tina were trying on makeup while I lined up a photo shoot of the two of them laughing. They looked so beautiful and free, and I wanted to show them later how I saw them. Even at 12 I could tell that girls needed to hear that sort of thing. I was beginning to feel awkward in my own body and I wanted us all to be confident like our moms. Like the women in the magazines.

When the girls finished their makeup, they did mine, and Tina grabbed the camera to turn it on me, noting I was barely in any of the photos. After a couple shots she asked Penny to take a photo of the Cousins, so I could frame it. We girls smiled with our arms around each other. Blue eye shadow, a bit too much eyeliner, and lipstick thick at our mouths, we felt beautiful.

Timeless.

Chapter 10

I woke up Friday morning just knowing it was going to be a bad day. I missed David a lot. Honestly, I was mad, so mad that he left us again. Not at him, just, frustrated at the situation. After so many years of it, I was just over military separations.

I knew it was hard on Lexi too. Before she knew how to talk about it Lexi used to cry and refuse to go to school. She would have tummy aches, or she'd get in trouble. She would yell at me and cry and scream and finally when she'd broken down so severely, she and I would sit on the couch and cry. We'd sit in the feelings together and wait until we'd exhausted our tears.

It got easier as Lexi got older. We created our own habits and traditions, like watching a movie on Friday nights with pizza and ice cream. We'd snuggle in and for that bit of time it all felt ok. But inevitably, as soon as the movie was over and it was time for bed, the sadness came back.

David missed birthdays, and holidays. We often had to celebrate something on an adjacent day or even an adjacent month because of his work schedule.

But Lexi and I didn't care much for resentment. We always knew it wasn't his fault. The job tells him what to do, and where to be, when to be there, and when he can leave. I never faulted Lexi for being angsty about it though. It was tough to be a teen. It was tough to be a human.

I left a note on the counter before heading in to work. Lexi was still sleeping, or was at the very least sitting in her bed texting and scrolling on her phone and hadn't emerged from her room yet. "Movie night?"

the note asked. I figured if I was feeling sad she probably was too. I had work, and I wasn't even sure what Lexi did with her time during the day other than daily coffee at The Cup. It'd been about two weeks since we'd moved in, and my job took a lot more time than I'd originally assumed it would.

Of course my mother told me it's ridiculous to work, since we didn't have to pay for rent or utilities, but I like to make my own way. I'm not used to being coddled, and I refused to let Dottie take away my independence. I also thought I'd lose my mind having nothing to do in a small town where I'd been actively avoiding everyone I had ever known.

But I loved movie nights. Lexi and I often counted on each other to raise the spirits of the day. David was so much fun when he was home, always organizing some sort of trip or activity, but we realized it was a different kind of fun when he was away.

Mom and daughter time warmed my heart, and I cherished it deeply.

WHEN I WALKED BACK into Wild Rose House on my lunch break, after a long morning of budgets and interviews, I saw an old cardboard box on the counter with my name written in black marker. Dottie's handwriting. I opened the box and carefully sifted through the contents.

I picked up a photo–the frame cracked on one corner–and sighed. I saw my 12-year-old self with my cousins Lauren and Tina, arms around each other, laughing and beautiful. Our makeup was a mess, but we were so happy. Penny had taken the photo, so she wasn't in it, but I knew if I turned the frame around I'd see all four names written on the back, with hearts and smiley faces all around them.

The photo had lived on the cluttered desk in my bedroom until the day I moved out, when I'd boxed up everything, deciding what to take and what to leave for my mother to deal with. I had every little detail of that photo and frame memorized. It had been the last thing I placed into the box designated to sit in the closet with the rest of the things I decided unnecessary for my new life. Sighing deeply and feeling the weight of the memory, I set the frame aside.

Under the photo was a mess of scrapbooks, folders, a friendship necklace, journals—all things I had forgotten about and at one time would have rather burned than see again. My mother had saved it all these years, knowing I hadn't been ready to deal with it. But why would she bring it out now? Nothing had changed. And somehow, I felt it—everything was different.

I breathed out one more deep sigh, letting the emotions flow through me before shaking them off. Seeing the photos made me extremely happy and nostalgic, but also deeply, to the bone, sad. I wanted to sort through everything in the box, and show my daughter all the people I grew up with and loved. But I had shared none of it with Lexi. I hadn't told her anything about my cousins, the beautiful summers at Wild Rose House, or the most awful summer of my life.

And I just wasn't ready to go there yet.

I quickly closed up the box and shoved it into my bedroom closet, throwing a sweatshirt and my nice dress heels on top of it, covering it. I'd metaphorically closed it off for so many years and I was ready to hide the physical memories again too.

Only, throughout the night, as I ate pizza and laughed with Lexi at the dumbest rom com movie we'd ever seen, I thought about the box. I thought about my cousins. It wouldn't leave my mind the way it usually did, most likely because of where I was sitting.

The furniture had changed, and the flooring was new, but some things would stay the same forever.

Chapter 11

1995

Tina sat on the floor at my feet, painting her toenails a pretty soft pink. Penny curled her legs up on the couch beside me. Lauren had the recliner, and Ty was facing upside down, staring at the ceiling, his legs on the couch beside Penny, who was trying not to let her annoyance show.

It was movie night at Wild Rose House and us almost-teenagers were watching the new Lion King VHS. We rode our bikes down to the movie rental shop and spent almost 30 minutes trying to decide which movie to watch. Just like always, everyone had different opinions. Tyler wanted to watch Airheads. The girls said no; it sounded too dumb. Lauren wanted to watch Forrest Gump. Dottie said no; it sounded too mature. There wasn't much to choose from anyway, with it being a Friday night in a town known for having nothing to do.

So Lion King was the compromise. It was secretly my choice, anyway, so I was happy about it, even though Tyler grumbled loudly during the entire previews.

I cried when Simba's dad died. I wondered what it'd be like to feel that pain, watching someone go away forever. Ty made fun of me and I threw a couch pillow at him.

"Ty, I swear, you better hope you never have to lose anyone someday and know what it feels like! How dare you make fun of Jenna!" Penny was always the first to stand up for her friends. I smiled weakly and told her it's ok. It embarrassed me when she did that, just as it embarrassed me when I cried in front of people.

"No one you know has ever died either," Ty yelled at Penny. She told him her dad had left when she was little and he said it wasn't the same thing. I hated when they fought with each other.

"Just finish watching, Penny," I told her. "It's just a movie. I'm obviously fine, and we're all sorry you don't have a dad."

We finished the rest of the movie in relative silence and cheered at the end for all the happy animals. I was still a little shaken by my emotional response. I vowed to be tougher in the future. I hated when Ty made fun of me, like he was so perfect and mature.

"Ty, what are you DOING?" I yelled after him as he ran into the kitchen. He came back with ice cream containers and spoons.

"I'm getting ice cream," he called back, smiling devilishly. I knew he was just trying to make up for hurting my feelings earlier. I'd allow it, I thought with a smirk, and caught a spoon he threw to me.

"Just don't tell Dottie we ate it all," I said. "She'll probably forget we even had it if we can all stick to the story."

They all looked at Penny. Penny always cracked first.

"Don't look at me!" she said. "I keep secrets all the time."

Everyone rolled their eyes and reached for spoons.

"I call the chocolate!" Ty yelled, snatching the container away while Tina reached for it, giggling at his quick ability to keep it from her.

Of all the times we spent together in our childhood summers, movie nights were definitely my favorite.

Chapter 12

Lexi was at her desk writing an email to her dad Saturday afternoon when I walked into the room and melted onto the bed. I picked at a quilt square and groaned.

"Your grandmother is infuriating," I started with a sigh. I was silent for a moment and then sat up, as if I was winding up for a long-winded rant. But just as quick as I sat up, I laid back down again, deflating in defeat.

"Sometimes I'm not sure why we're here."

Lexi raised an eyebrow in question and smirked the snarkiest teen smirk she could. She'd literally been asking that question every day since we got there.

"I knew it would be hard," I started again. "I did. It's my old home, and it's my 40-year-old self basically living with my parents. I didn't expect it to be easy! But she wants to control every single little thing, and I can't do it, Lexi."

Lexi laughed and told me she's so sorry, her voice dripping with sarcasm. I suppose she knows a little something about parents controlling every aspect of their daughter's life.

But instead of saying that, she plopped onto the bed next to me. Sometimes when there's nothing to be said, being there is enough. She wrapped her arms around me and let me sulk.

"I don't know why I'm the one saying this, but you know we'll be ok," Lexi stated maturely. "We'll get through the deployment, and this weird town, and grama's quilting circle and book club and church socials..."

She paused a moment, remembering something she hadn't told me.

"But we might not get through whatever is living in that cornfield, Mom. Seriously, what's in there? I haven't believed in monsters under my bed or in my closet since I was 4, but I swear there are monsters in that field. I heard something rustling in the stalks last night!"

I laughed and hugged my daughter tight.

"Thank you, love. I needed a good pick me up. You're right, we're going to get through this and we're going to be better for it." I stood up and took a deep breath, obviously feeling a little lighter, and winked. "But honestly, don't go in there."

Chapter 13

1996

The summer I turned 13 was wilder than the summers before. Tina and I decided we wanted to date boys and be in the cool group at school. We decided we WERE the cool group, and we wanted to be the ones deciding who would sit with us at lunch, and who would talk about us before school in the rotunda.

Lauren, a year older, coached us on how to dress, and how to act. She helped when we started our periods within 2 weeks of each other. She was our mentor, our friend, our guide through junior high. Everything would change now that we were 13, Tina predicted.

I hosted a backyard bonfire for my birthday that summer. I invited the usual Wild Rose crew. I also invited some girls from school and the boys we thought were cute, mostly Ty's friends. Ty of course hated the reasoning for their invites but he was more just glad he could have his cousins and his friends around at the same time for once, and having some extra girls who weren't related to him was something Ty was newly excited about as well.

Penny wasn't happy at the new changes, or at any changes, but she was too anxious to say anything. Every time she tried to hide it, I could see right through her, but I never let on that I knew. She pretended to like makeup, and tried to dress better, but her mom couldn't afford much so she would often take hand-me-downs from Lauren and me. Penny was probably the prettiest of all the girls but she was just odd and didn't seem to want any extra attention; she just wanted to fit in with us. She wanted things to stay the same, which meant being silly and happy at childhood things, not trying to look like or act like adults.

"If only you'd just try, Penny," I would tell her. "Look, we can curl your hair, and if you'd just add some blush..." We'd spend hours critiquing each other's looks, sifting through teen magazines and comparing ourselves to the models and celebrities in the photos. I felt a little bad about it, because I honestly thought we were pretty just as we were, but I wanted to be cool like Lauren, and I wanted a boyfriend who would look at me the way the boys looked at girls in the movies.

That night we were sitting beside the bonfire that my dad had built. Charles and Dottie were hanging off to the side of the yard, always trying to be close for safety but far enough to give me some space. They were still too close, I thought. I sat next to Brian, and Tina had told me he'd planned on holding my hand when it got dark. I didn't need my parents ruining it.

I pushed my hand over closer to him just in case he needed a hint, and he put his fingers over mine. We looked at each other and I blushed, and he asked if it was ok if we held hands. I nodded, my cheeks pink. I hoped it looked like I was warm from the fire.

A few minutes later I looked around for Tina and didn't see her. "Where's Tina?" I asked Brian quietly. I didn't want to get her in trouble, but I needed to know she was ok. I'd had what the girls called cousin intuition.

Brian shrugged and said he thought she went into the field.

"Shoot, the field?" I asked, panicking a bit. The corn wasn't tall yet, but we weren't supposed to go into the field, ever, unless we were with an adult.

I tapped Penny and whispered I needed help, trying not to alert the parents. Together we snuck into the back where I hoped I'd find my cousin.

"Tina?" I whispered loudly. "Tina, I need to know where you are right now!"

Tina called out from somewhere that she was ok, she was just with Mike. I rolled my eyes and told her to get back out from there and join the party. She definitely shouldn't be alone with Mike. Her parents would flip out if they knew we girls had snuck off.

When Tina stubbornly wouldn't come back, I got worried and went after her, squinting in the darkness, trying to follow my cousin's voice as she giggled and talked with Mike. Then Penny followed me, promising to stay with me. We girls knew better than to leave each other alone. Lauren wasn't with us, but we needed her back at the fire to keep us from getting in trouble.

We stepped in between the cornstalks and whisper-yelled for Tina to come out. I had to go in further to reach my cousin. We walked ahead slowly, step by step, trying to be mindful of our foot placement.

"OUCH!" I yelled suddenly, cursing. "Dangit, guys, I think something bit me." I turned and looked at Penny, wide eyed, and yelled for everyone to run back to the group.

We all ran back to the bonfire together then, crying, screaming, and then laughing. I hadn't gotten bitten; I just scratched and poked my leg on a cornstalk. But the story for the rest of the summer was how I bravely rescued my cousin, who'd been "lost" in the field.

We'd done it. We'd gotten our story, and our schoolmates thought we were so brave, and so cool. Everyone believed the story all summer long. Until Penny ratted us out, eventually.

That's one more reason we said she could never could keep a secret.

Chapter 14

"Toss me a sammy, please," Sophie yelled to Lexi. She threw the homemade peanut butter and chocolate chip sandwich to her friend and grabbed one for herself too. Their small cooler also held Diet Coke and orange Jell-O, their collective favorite, as well as a smattering of chocolate and sour candies.

We'd all been at the "beach" for about an hour, enjoying the sun and sand with a few local adults and high schoolers roaming in and out around them. The county brought in the sand at the beginning of summer, and replenished it annually, so it was always pretty and clean.

It'd been decades since I'd relaxed on the lake beach. I told Lexi no one actually swims, because the water usually held a plethora of things no one wanted to invite into their body, and I don't think she believed me until Sophie backed me up. The water on that particular Saturday was cloudy and green and looked like a bacteria fest. I wore a romper that Lexi almost forbade me to leave the house in, stating it's about time I dress for my age. She'd worn her bikini with a sundress over top, and we had matching silver flip flops. We were just fine on the plastic and metal folding layout chairs we'd swiped from Wild Rose House. Sophie had a similar chair, and we'd gone early to set up at a decent spot. The teens had spent the last hour gossiping about the townspeople, Lexi's friends in San Antonio, and the boys and girls they'd go to high school with in just a couple short months.

The sky was blue and slightly overcast, and old-school skate punk music was playing on a speaker somewhere far enough away to hear but not close enough to mess with their conversation. The day was perfect, and exactly what Lexi and I had needed. I'd felt bad tagging along with the teens but Lexi told me I needed time away from my job and she'd make an exception just this once. Still, I tried to stay on the edge of their group so they could talk without fear of a mom judging and listening in. Obviously I was listening in though.

"So what's with the hearing aids, friends? It's so weird you both have them," a girl named Emmy asked, sitting on a towel in the sand between Lexi and Sophie. "Sorry, I don't mean weird, but it's just strange you both have them when no one else we know does. You know what I mean? What's it like being deaf?"

Lexi and Sophie looked at each other, and Sophie nodded, signaling she'd answer for them. I know from experience they both probably got the question a lot.

"Well, Emmy, it's a lot like being not deaf, except I can't hear sometimes."

Lexi and Sophie laughed while Emmy giggled nervously.

"Seriously, Emmy, it's not a big deal," Sophie continued. "I have this syndrome that affects my hearing. It's a progressive loss, which means I'll lose it all someday. I'll either get cochlear implant surgery or I'll learn to live with the silence and use sign language or whatever."

Lexi gasped. "I have that same syndrome! What do you think you'll do? I'll get the CI surgery for sure. I can't live without music."

Emmy agreed and cracked a joke about wishing she could live without Mr. Thompson's stupid voice in world geography. My mind lingered on the syndrome my daughter and Sophie shared, and I instantly wondered who's parents were. The two could be twins, they looked so much alike. Those green eyes...

"For REAL!" Sophie agreed and dodged a foam football sliding by her head before I could ask any more about her life. I wasn't supposed to be listening in, anyway. "DUDE! Watch the head!" she yelled to someone.

The owner of the football jogged over, barefoot in the hot sand, to retrieve it. "Hi Sophie," he said to her shyly.

She rolled her eyes and said hi back, tossing him the foam ball and turning back to the girls beside her. He jogged off, turning to look behind him, trying to catch Sophie's eyes one more time before heading back to his friends. I bit my lip to stop laughing at the pure teenageness of the interaction.

"Jake's sweet but he's so dumb," she said, laughing. "Cute though, right?" She grabbed her phone and snapped a picture of the guys tossing the ball to each other. After posting it to the socials and tagging them, she turned to the girls and asked them to crowd in for a selfie.

"It's a SELfie," she said to them, snapping the photo as they looked at her, confused. I closed my eyes and let the sun relax me, trying hard not to let my own memories overtake me. "Shoot, do it again, weirdos. You know, SEL—Sophie, Emmy, Lexi." She pushed the camera icon again as the three of them cracked up laughing. It felt like a defining moment, with the three of them. The beginning of something. I wanted Lexi to lock the memory away forever and cherish it during all the times she felt lonely and like she didn't fit in. I wanted to lock the memory in my own mind; I was so proud of the young woman my daughter was becoming and it was awesome seeing how comfortable she was in her new friend group.

Later in her journal to her dad Lexi would mention the moment and tell him she was cautiously planting those roots he'd asked of her. She'd attach the photo, and he'd write back telling her how genuinely happy and radiant she looks.

"OUCH" Lexi yelled. The foam football was at it again, this time hitting Lexi's thigh with an impressive speed. I smirked, having seen this game before. A boy she hadn't noticed before ran over to ask for it back. I watched her hold up the ball, scrunching her face from the bright sun. It was like a movie scene, the boy in front of her, smiling with perfect white teeth, the sun behind him creating a sort of halo effect. She playfully shook her head and rolled her eyes and he smiled bigger, accepting the ball and thanking her with a goofy salute before jogging back to the guys.

She continued to stare, and Emmy pushed her playfully and told her to come back to earth. I adjusted my sun hat and looked away, trying not to embarrass her.

"I see you've met Matty," Emmy said, winking to Sophie. "He's great, right?" Lexi blushed and smirked at her new friend.

"Yeah, he's, um, athletic," she stammered, smoothing her pink braids and sneaking a look at herself using her cellphone camera. I could see her glance at me but I closed my eyes and turned my head, hoping she'd feel a sense of privacy.

"I hope I played that cool," she groaned. "In front of my mom too!" She looked mortified, and I shrugged my shoulders, smirking again. Sophie laughed and told Lexi I'm so much cooler than her own mom, who would do something super cringey like ask him who his mother is and why she didn't teach him manners. I smiled and winked, choosing to keep my mouth closed at the compliment. I reminded myself I was meant to be the quiet tagalong mother, not the journalist.

Matty and Lexi, I thought. This also felt like the beginning of something big.

For a relaxing Saturday, I had more anxiety by the end of the day than I did at the beginning.

Chapter 15

"Kaitlyn, I need you to go down to Jefferson Street and get me as much as you can on the empty lot. They've got walls going up and we need to know what's going in there. Josh, you're on sports so I need to know what everyone's got going as we're getting ready for school starting up again. Practices, game schedules, coach bios, whatever you can find, ok?"

I was exhausted, but giving assignments to the new staff members, all two of them, felt amazing. I was so happy to have them, even if they had little experience.

"Um, Jenna? You want me to write an article on a wall?" Kaitlyn clarified.

I smiled and laughed lightly, remembering back to my early days of reporting on odd small town stories.

"It's a wall now, but it's going to turn into something," I told the young employee. "It's our job to let people know what's happening, and in a small town, that means often reporting on empty lots. I promise it won't always be walls, my friend, now go on and bust that story!"

I was actually loving my new role, and I felt like I was pretty good at it. We'd scheduled our first printing—the first for which I was fully in charge—for Friday, just 3 days away. Eventually we would have a small website, but for now we just wanted to keep from folding so we focused on the printed newspaper and free social media accounts.

After dismissing the writers to their assignments, I turned to my new intern, Callie, amazed I'd been able to get this program going so quickly. Apparently Mr. Smith had a longstanding intern program with the high school and normally had a student every summer help for class credit. Poor Callie had been waiting to see if she had a job or not, and I was extremely grateful she'd been waiting in the wings.

We'd been working on how to layout a newspaper on the computer. I'd taught the teen how to drop the story into the design software, along with the coordinating photos, and how to edit for space. I was nervous putting all this on a high school student but Callie took it all in and delivered quick and almost flawless results.

"Let's fix this headline. It's not long enough for the space. See how it looks like that? Let's make it say... 'The Cup Runneth Over with Donations'... yes, I know it's cheesy. Welcome to small-town news, kid," I said with a laugh.

Working with the high school student, an incoming senior, made me miss my own incoming senior. I walked to my desk and sat down at my computer. The background was a photo of the three of us, David, Lexi and me, at a holiday party a few years ago in Utah. Mountains in the background, smiles so big full teeth were showing. We'd been so happy.

I was happy now too, but it was just not the same. I missed David, for sure, but being in my hometown made me miss my family immensely. I kept thinking I'd run into everyone and we'd make plans to do a movie night at Wild Rose House. Lauren would bring cookie dough. Ty and Tina would show up arguing but would toss me a pack of Sour Patch Kids before going back to their twin conversation. Penny would show up late with a story and a hug that would let me know our sisterhood was real, that everything was special and exactly as it should be. I knew it could never happen, but sometimes I felt as though I would turn around and see them all waiting, together and happy.

I looked around at my office, at its white painted walls and old industrial feel. This had been Willow's newspaper building since the beginning of time, I thought. There were no true offices with doors. Everyone had desks and spaces for their privacy in thinking, planning, and writing. But it was open enough that everyone could yell across the room when they needed help with something. It had barely changed since the time my class took a field trip in 5th grade, with students looking around in awe, thinking about being adults with real jobs. Back then there was a full staff and people bustling around back and forth, looking for files and calling people on corded phones to clarify quotes and details. Even for a small town it was a large scale operation with so many moving parts. It seemed so glamorous and important to me as a 5th grader, and it seemed just as glamorous and important to me now as an adult.

There used to be a small printing press in the back, but everything gets outsourced now. Sometimes I liked to go back to where the press used to stand and imagine the bustling daily news schedule, people rushing all over trying to get the inked information to the masses every morning before most of the town even woke up for the day.

"Jenna?" someone called out, snapping me back to attention. An older woman from a business down the street had walked in with a camera in her hand. "I have photos of the new butterfly garden at the hospital. Did you get any? I know you're still trying to get everything going here. I've been helping Mr. Smith for a while, taking photos whenever I'm out. My daughter and grandson gave me this beautiful camera for my birthday a few years ago."

Small towns were infuriating with their "everyone in your business" ways, but sometimes that was the very thing that made them amazing. I drew out a breath, thankful for the extra and unexpected help.

"Thank you, Mrs. Jones!" I exclaimed, rushing to see what she offered. "These are so helpful! Let me get you cash for those. You'll get photo credit in the paper too."

The woman brushed me off. She wouldn't accept money for photos she would have taken anyway, she explained.

"Mrs. Jones, you are a saint!" I exclaimed, thinking about the budget that didn't fully exist yet. "I can't wait to get these in before printing!"

As Mrs. Jones gave me the SD card to plug into my computer, she glanced at the computer screen and lit up at seeing the background picture.

"Is that your daughter?" she exclaimed. "I almost didn't recognize her without her pink hair. I see her at the coffee shop almost every day. Such a sweet girl, that Lexi. I love seeing her with Lauren's girl, the snarky one who serves coffee. They remind me so much of you and Lauren at that age!"

I almost dropped the SD card as I handed it back to her, shocked at the mention of Lauren and the daughter I didn't know she had. Suddenly everything made sense, and I felt a new sense of guilt. Lexi and Sophie were cousins. Lauren still lived in Willow. The air seemed to leave my lungs and my head turned fuzzy, so I just nodded.

"I need to get back to work, dear," she continued, squeezing my hand. "I'm glad I could help with the butterfly garden story. Please let me know if I can do anything else. We're sure happy to have you and Lexi here with us this summer. It's good to have you back. We all feel that way."

She squeezed my hand once more and left the building, but her words and the ghost of the past still lingered long after the room was clear.

Chapter 16

"Mom, I'm heading out!" Lexi yelled through my bedroom door. I opened the door, hoping she didn't realize I'd been pacing back and forth, waiting for her to be ready. I met her in the hall as she grabbed her purse and checked her reflection in the hallway mirror. She added some lip gloss and fluffed her long hair, curled for the occasion and sitting loose around her shoulders. She was beautiful and confident and I was an anxious mess.

"Have a good time, and be safe!" I told her. Matty was going to be there any minute to pick her up for their first date and Lexi did not want him to run into Dottie on the way. She hoped to meet him at the front and avoid any embarrassment.

"Please, just let me go quietly," Lexi begged. I had my phone up and was waiting to take a photo of our daughter's "first Iowa date" to share with David. Lexi smiled obediently and hurried out the door. She got to the driveway just as Matty was pulling up in a freshly washed but beat up old pickup truck.

She opened the car door before he could get out and I couldn't hear what they said as she closed the door and buckled her seatbelt. I silently wished my kiddo the best of luck, as I know first dates can be tricky at that age. Everything's so dramatic and embarrassing, but also so fun and easy. I couldn't wait to hear all about it when she got home.

My phone dinged, and I worried when I saw Lexi's name pop up on the screen.

"Bowling," said the text, with a bunch of emojis showing headache and pain and eyerolls. Oh, the poor girl. I remembered taking Lexi bowling a bunch of times with David, and we'd always leave early with an overwhelmed and overstimulated kid. The noise was usually way too high for Lexi's hearing aids and she could never fully understand the conversation with so much commotion. I sighed and text her back: "Do your best! I'll have headache medicine waiting for you when you get home," and put my phone in my pocket.

I found a small bit of ice cream left in the freezer and shuffled to the couch, not sure what to do with my evening. I know what I didn't want to do is hang out with Dottie. I tried to read for a bit, turning off the overhead lights and opting for soft lamps beside the couch. I must have dozed off because it was about an hour later when I heard the front door open.

"Shoot," Lexi cursed, running into the hall table on her way to the kitchen. She shouted out when she noticed me on the couch, still holding my e-reader.

"Mom, you scared me! What are you doing sitting in the dark?" She changed her course and sat down beside me.

"I was reading, and I fell asleep," I told her. "It wasn't this dark when I sat down. What are you doing home early? Bowling?"

She nodded. "Headache," she answered. "It was so loud in there. Why do people enjoy that? Do we have any ice cream?"

I looked over to the empty container and sighed an apology. She shrugged and got up to search the freezer for more.

"I hid this behind the frozen peas for a reason," she said to me, winking. We sat on the couch together, eating ice cream, discussing whose night was lamer, when I asked her about Sophie.

"What's she like?" I asked nonchalantly. I'd really only seen her a couple times, once at the coffee shop and once at the beach. She seemed a lot like my daughter and I was intrigued at the thought of Lauren and me being pregnant at the same 17 years ago time and not even knowing.

"Oh, well..." she thought. "I mean, you met her, and she's pretty much exactly what you saw. We have a lot in common. We both have green eyes and wear hearing aids. Coffee is life. Music is only good when it's our choice. Bowling sucks. Sand and sun is a good idea, even when it's just a lake beach."

She grabbed her phone.

"Did you see the selfie we took? I just love it. Emmy and Sophie look so happy here, right?" She shifted the phone so I could see the photo they took at the beach. It reminded me so much of the photo I saw in the box Dottie left for me. Three beautiful girls smiling like the world will never change, like the moment will last forever.

I had an urge to get up and go find the broken frame to share my own friendship moment with my daughter. I suddenly wanted to tell her everything. But Lexi asked me about my first real date, and reality set in what I'd almost done on a terrible whim. I wasn't ready, obviously.

I blinked hard, calling up the memory, and cringed just thinking about the time Brian took me to get pizza.

"Oh, no, you better buckle up, sister," I told her. "This one's a cringe fest."

Chapter 17

1996

I had never gone on an actual date before. After the bonfire with Brian, I realized I was ready. I'd been brave and had asked Brian if he wanted to go on a date and he said he'd have to ask his mom to drive us. She said ok, and that was that. My first boyfriend. My first date. I was a nervous wreck.

Brian's mom picked me up, chatting with Dottie for a few minutes while Brian and I awkwardly fidgeted, not sure how to act or what to say. We shyly said hello to each other, and Brian thanked Dottie for allowing her daughter to go. He promised to be nice and that we'd be home on time. I could see Dottie trying not to smile, nodding politely and motioning to go ahead and get in the car. The whole thing was embarrassing.

The ride to the restaurant was quiet. Brian asked me if I like pizza, and I said yes. I didn't know what else to say, so I looked out the window at the trees and sidewalks whizzing by.

We pulled the car into the crowded parking lot of a favorite local pizza restaurant. Brian's mom told them she'd sit at another table, and she kept her promise, allowing us teens to sit in a booth together, the giant table in between us, making me feel small, like I was pretending to be grown up.

"Um, what kind of pizza do you like?" he asked me. "I like anything."

I answered quietly, telling him I like anything too, wanting to be accommodating. Brian lit up and told the server he'd "order for the table," choosing pepperoni and sausage pizza with cheese stuffed in the crust. "We'll splurge and have pop too please," he told her, looking at me for confirmation. I shrugged. I hated pepperoni—it was too greasy—and I really just wanted water. But I wanted Brian to like me so I said that was fine.

When we got our pop from the fountain, Brian tripped and spilled his Mountain Dew all over my back. I stood stiffly, not sure what to do, as his face turned bright red.

"I'm so sorry!" he yelled, looking around for napkins as I struggled to keep from crying. "Here, um, maybe you should go to the bathroom? I can get my mom."

Brian's mother calmly led me to the bathroom and helped me dry off with the electric hand dryer. I was in tears and struggled to shrug it off, smiling to thank her for helping.

When we got back to the table, the pizza was already there. Brian had already started eating, but when he saw my mouth drop in shock, he had the decency to look embarrassed.

"I didn't want it to get cold..." he started. Brian's mom rolled her eyes and told me to go ahead and enjoy my pizza and let her know if I needed anything else. She gave her son a look of annoyance and went back to her table.

I picked off all the pepperoni, ate my pizza in silence, and waited patiently for Brian to say something. When he didn't, I asked how his summer was going—anything to fill the silence.

This was not the date I wanted. I'd rather be back at Wild Rose House playing checkers with Tina, yelling at Ty to stop taking all the pieces because we still needed them.

I sighed and looked toward the door. As if summoned because I'd thought about them, Tina and Ty walked in with their mom, waiting in the pickup line for their pizza to go.

Tina narrowed her eyes when she saw me with Brian. I'd found out after the bonfire that Tina had been crushing on Brian and had only run off to the cornfield with Mike in jealousy, after seeing us hold hands.

At that moment I wanted to rush over and laugh with Tina about my horrible night, and tell her she definitely shouldn't crush on Brian because he was awkward and embarrassing and didn't know how to carry on a conversation. He wasn't good enough for her and I wished I'd never gone on the date at all. But Brian chose that exact minute to reach over the table and hold my hand. I just stared at our hands, intertwined, and grimaced.

"I'm sorry tonight was bad," he said to me, sheepish. "Can we maybe just start over? I have two quarters if you want to go play the race car game." I smiled at him and peeked over to the door again to see Tina storming outside, Ty behind her yelling at her to slow down.

I sighed and looked at my date. "Sure, Brian, let's go play the race car game," I told him, and his face lit up again. We had a decent time playing. I let him win most of the games. By the time Brian's mom told us it was time to go, I had mostly forgiven him for the pop incident. And really, how was he supposed to know about my pizza if I didn't tell him? He was a nice boy, I decided, so when he wanted to hold my hand on the way to the car, I decided I wanted it too.

I just wished I could call Tina and tell her all about it. I wondered quietly on the way home how I could fix everything between us.

Chapter 18

The lights twinkled red, white and blue, and streamers attached to the backs of chairs swayed slightly in the breeze. The 4th of July parade would begin soon and I was of course covering the story for the paper. I'd already interviewed those in charge and got some quotes from people in the crowd. My intern Cassie, a flute player, would march with the band, and the other staffers set up in various spots with cameras and notepads. I would rely on the public to send in photos of the things I'd miss, like face painting and the pie-eating contest.

I looked around to see if I could find Lexi among the crowd at the coffee shop. My daughter had gotten a job working at The Cup, since she was there almost daily anyway, but was very short with the rest of her conversation the last couple days, always running off somewhere else. We both stayed busy, me with the paper and town meetings and Lexi with her job, friends, and boyfriend, but I couldn't help but wonder if there was another reason for her absence. Lexi had always gone distant when something was on her mind, and I felt awful about my busy schedule barely allowing for the two of us to cross paths, let alone have a conversation the last couple days. I made a mental note to plan another mother daughter movie night, and forced my mind back into work mode.

Walking around, snapping photos and taking notes, I got closer to The Cup, where I could see Lexi and Sophie laughing, clapping, and pointing at floats as they passed. They looked so much alike and it was lovely to see them together, but it also worried me, as I had yet to talk to my daughter about my own past and her connection with her new best friend.

It was too loud to yell hello but eventually I caught Sophie's eye and waved. I pointed to Lexi and Sophie turned to elbow her friend. Lexi waved too and then signed that we'd talk later. I signed O-K back and went on around the square, capturing as much of the excitement as possible. The Independence Day event went fast and packed a punch and the 4th of July double issue would be a big moneymaker. We'd sold a lot of ads for this issue and I wanted to make the most of it. The town was counting on me to deliver and I didn't want to disappoint them.

As I circled around to the backside of the courthouse, I ran—literally—into my old friend Penny, who had been watching the floats with, wouldn't you know it, Lauren. I recognized her instantly, even though it'd been 2 decades since I'd seen her. She matured a little but otherwise hadn't changed a bit.

"Wow, look Penny, it's Jenna! She ran right into you like she didn't even see you..." Lauren said to Penny before raising her eyebrow at me. She sighed and composed her face. "How are you, Jenna? It's been a while..."

We hugged awkwardly and exchanged pleasantries, even though Lauren looked at me like I smelled. I deserved it; I knew. I looked at Penny, whose face scrunched up like she was holding in a secret. She started tapping her foot and blew out a breath before spurting out, "Lexi and Sophie know they're cousins."

Lauren smiled almost wickedly, and I gasped, trying to remind myself it was inevitable. The small-town gossip was bound to overflow with information like that, especially once anyone who knew anything saw them together. It was silly to think someone wouldn't tell them, since the two of them no doubt reminded people from the old days of Lauren and me. People probably didn't even realize it had been a secret. It shouldn't have been a secret, I thought to myself.

"Well, I suppose they would have found out, eventually," I said slowly, my brain trying to catch up with all the quick developments. "Lauren, they look like sisters," I told my cousin, reaching out to touch her arm. I let out a deep breath. "It's good to see you. You look just the same."

Lauren rolled her eyes but gave a little pose, a smile touching her lips. At 41, she looked as though she'd spent quite a bit of money and effort to stay young looking. I assumed weekly trips to the spa and expensive skin care helped Lauren protect her youthful glow.

"Lauren's a realtor," Penny announced. "That's why she looks so businessy. She used to have an ad run in the newspaper, but I guess she doesn't anymore or you would have seen it!"

It'd been over 20 years since we'd seen each other. My high school graduation was the last time, and we'd spoken on the phone only a couple times after that, with basic announcements about getting married. Our short conversations had been too awkward, so we'd stopped communicating altogether. I hadn't known about her pregnancy and if she'd known about mine, it was only because of Dottie.

It was fate our daughters had run into each other in the cafe the first week we'd moved in, I knew, and I wasn't about to ruin that, but I knew the time for secrets was ending quickly. My daughter would make a wonderful journalist if she'd wanted to—and she would get this whole story if she wanted it, if she hadn't already.

"Penny, how much do they know?" I looked at my friend, knowing Penny was no doubt the reason for the truth coming out.

"I don't know, Jen, maybe you should just sit down and talk to her," Penny said with a sigh. "Maybe sit down with all of us. I'm just as confused as anyone. I get why you left, but I don't know why you had to stay away for so long. If we could all just get over this whole thing, I think you'd see we're all still here for you. We could be the same again."

I put a hand up, cutting Penny off, and looked around to see who was listening for gossip. "It'll never be the same, Pen. You know that. Thank you for looking out for my girl. I appreciate that so very much. She's been through a lot in her life so far and it means the world to me seeing her happy and letting people in. She's usually SO closed off and scared to make friends. Lauren, your daughter has given mine someone to relate to, and I won't do anything at all to jeopardize that. But I can't do this right now. I'm working, and I just... I can't. I will call you soon. I promise."

I smiled weakly at them both, reached out to touch their arms in an almost group hug, and stopped short, turning instead to walk away.

I had her story to write. This family drama would have to wait.

Chapter 19

1997

Teenage summers in the 90s seemed to slide along in a blur of earning money, swimming, hanging out at Wild Rose House, and anything and everything having to do with boys.

I had stayed with Brian the past year even though I hadn't really wanted to; he was kind and sweet and didn't cause me drama, but I knew it wasn't love. We went to the movies sometimes, and to get pizza with his mom. Dottie drove us to get ice cream after our soccer practice. We sat together at lunch. It wasn't serious, but we had enjoyed each other's company the past however many months.

I'd finally broken up with him before the school year ended and as expected, he didn't take it too hard. "OK," he said, and shrugged before running off to play football with his friends. As easily as it started, it ended. My first relationship hadn't ended in heartbreak and for that I was thankful.

I wanted that summer, the summer of 14, to be about the Wild Rose Girls. I missed hanging out with Penny, Lauren, and Tina. I missed painting Ty's toenails when he fell asleep sprawled out on the sofa, and watching Nickelodeon and Disney Channel until we fell asleep too. I missed begging one of our moms to drive us to the pool, and riding our bikes to the candy store, unloading coins we'd found stuck in the couch cushions.

I wanted that summer to be special, and I was determined to bring them all back together after the year of school and busy schedules separating us.

So I invited everyone over for a slumber party the weekend after school let out. I tried to ask Ty too, but he was leaving for football camp and he said he wouldn't be caught dead with painted toenails again. I'd caught up with him at lunch and told him he was being silly for not trusting me, and he tousled my hair and called me a liar before laughing and running off.

I'd planned the slumber party perfectly. Dottie bought sleeping bags and new pillows for everyone that summer, to be kept as "house linens". Penny's blanket had been threadbare the last time she'd been over, and no one wanted her to feel badly about not having things her friends had. My mom always did little things to make everyone feel equal, and I know Penny especially appreciated it. I had Dottie put ice cream in the freezer and filled the fridge with pop and Lunchables. I begged my mom to rent the new Romeo and Juliet but we'd probably just watch whatever was playing on tv instead. We used commercial breaks as timers for grabbing snacks and doing bathroom breaks.

When everyone came, I could hardly contain my excitement.

"I am so glad you're all here!" I exclaimed, bringing them in for a group hug. I gave them a tour of the goods and handed them each a can of Mountain Dew, Diet for Lauren, who was experimenting with the unfortunate diet culture of the time. We talked about our last days of school and complained about the end of the year testing. Lauren, always a year older, told us which of the 8th grade teachers were cool and which bathroom was the "good one".

We had an awesome night. It was just the bonding we girls needed to set the tone for the rest of the summer. Penny suggested we swear off boys until school started again and though there was a little grumbling we all nodded in agreement and pinky swore to focus on our friendship instead. Boys would come and go but our friendship would be forever.

Chapter 20

After the mess of emotions brought on by the 4th of July parade, I was happy to have a day away from everyone in Willow. Lexi and I headed up to the big city of Des Moines for Lexi's audiology appointment and some mom-daughter shopping. It'd been a while since we'd wandered a mall and we were ready–comfy clothes, Chucks on our feet, and money in our wallets.

We got lost on the way to the audiology office—even with turn by turn navigation—and by the time we got there we had to run in to make it in time. As fate would have it, we passed a familiar set of cousins in the lobby heading out. Sometimes I had to laugh at the audacity of the universe.

Lexi stopped short of literally pushing into Sophie. "Oh, hey!" she told her. "I would say funny running into you here, but actually it's about the only place outside of Willow that makes sense." She winked and gave her a quick hug.

Lauren looked at the two girls and drew in a sharp breath. No doubt she was probably noticing how alike they look standing together.

"Jenna, hi, I can see you're on your way to your appointment. Are you doing lunch or shopping after? We could meet you when you're done." She paused and raised an eyebrow, trying to see through my facade to figure out what I really thought about us spending some time together. "The girls would love to pick out some back to school clothes together and I know you and I could use the time to catch up."

I seized with anxiety and fear, but the teens both exclaimed, "Yes!" before quietly giggling, remembering where they were. "Please Mom, just say yes so we can go!" Lexi begged. I nodded, knowing they caught me, and reminded my daughter we were running late.

We made quick plans to meet at the food court of the mall nearby and then Lexi and I rushed to check in while Lauren and Sophie left the office.

Audiology appointments were always pretty standard for Lexi. She's had them every six months since she was 2 years old, and though her hearing fluctuated a bit from time to time, it always stayed pretty stable. This appointment was no surprise.

"Easy peasy," Lexi said once she finished testing and getting new tubes fitted for her hearing aids. "Now let's go please," she begged, pulling on my arm like she used to as a toddler. I settled with the front desk, made the next appointment, and we girls were on our way. The mall was a few minutes down the road and I saw Lexi texting furiously in her seat on the passenger side of the SUV.

"Lexi," I started, watching the road but side eyeing her to make sure she heard me. "I know you figured out that you and Sophie are cousins, and I don't know why you haven't said anything about it yet." I hesitated before continuing. "Are you mad I didn't tell you? I only just found out myself, but I really do want to talk about it when you're ready."

The teen fidgeted with her pink braid and shrugged.

"I sort of figured there was a reason you didn't want to tell me, or maybe you didn't realize who she was at first and it's weird for you, and I'm waiting for you to realize that I'm ready for whatever else it is you think you're hiding so well." She looked at me before answering another text, smiling at the message on the screen. She adjusted her face to a scowl and said, "I'm not a little kid, you know? I can handle it. Whatever happened with you and Lauren, Sophie and I can deal with it."

It was quiet in the car as we pulled into the parking garage. I found a spot, turned off the vehicle, and unbuckled her seatbelt, turning to face my daughter.

"Lauren is my cousin, and my oldest friend," I started. "Things haven't been right between us for more years than they were right. I just didn't want you to get your hopes up if she and I didn't want a relationship. I wasn't even sure she still lived in Willow. That's why I didn't tell you about her. I didn't have any sisters. At one time Lauren was like an older sister to me and I loved her dearly. I can see that same love with you and Sophie," I said, reaching out to touch Lexi's hand. "I wouldn't take that away for anything, sweetheart. Lauren and I will be fine. We'll find our way back. I don't want you to worry, but I also don't want you to mess with our process, ok? Give us some time."

We promised each other we'd honor each other's boundaries and gave a quick hug before finding our way into the mall and to the food court. We had work to do.

As we'd moved all around the United States, we'd realized there was always a mall around and always a food court. We had so many fun traditions; this one called for us each to each pick something from a different restaurant and share. Usually, the goal was to pick something unexpected and see how it worked together with everyone else's choices. Sometimes it was great and sometimes a complete gross mess, but it was always humorous and fun.

We filled in Lauren and Sophie on the tradition, and they instantly wanted to play along, shuffling off each in a different direction. When we came back together, we laughed at the ridiculous food on our trays. Chinese noodles, sausage and mushroom pizza, French fries, chocolate ice cream, a jalapeno cheeseburger, and frosted and sprinkled donuts.

"Mom, why would you get sausage and mushroom? We always get pepperoni!" Sophie chided her mom, grabbing a fry from Lexi's tray.

Lauren smiled and glanced at me, winking. "Not everyone likes pepperoni, dear," she answered her daughter.

My breath caught in my throat for a moment at the sweet thought, and I laughed as I struggled to recover, grabbing the pizza before anyone else could. "It's MINE," I said and took a large bite before signing "Thank you" to my cousin. Lauren winked again and dipped a fry in the chocolate ice cream.

"Nice choice on the ice cream flavor too," she told me. I knew chocolate was her favorite and yes I might have thought about that when I chose. "But Sophie, WHY did you get donuts?"

The blonde teen acted shocked and offended. "Ohhhhh, ok, I didn't know we had to have a REASON to buy DONUTS, Mom. Please..."

The afternoon went so well, with all four of us laughing and commenting how great the gene pool was in our family tree as we took a photo in front of a large fountain. We shopped, played in the arcade, got late afternoon coffee at Starbucks, and then realized we had to call it a night sometime.

"This went well," Lauren commented quietly, sliding her arm around me and tilting her head to mine. The familiar gesture took me off guard and I fought tears for the hundredth time. I nodded, clearing my throat to thank her for joining us. We were about to branch off to our own parking sections when the girls, who'd been whispering together, jumped up and agreed with something in unison.

"Mom, Mother, Mama, Mommy..." Lexi started. She waited until I popped a hand on my hip and gestured to her to go ahead. "We had the best idea ever and please don't say no ok? Can we have a bonfire at Wild Rose House? Maybe we can invite Emmy and some of the other kids who will be in school with me. It would be so great to be the cool girl starting out, right? And there is definitely a spot where I KNOW ya'll have done bonfires when you were young. Don't even deny it. Dottie told me."

I rolled my eyes and told her we'd discuss it, and Lauren said it sounded like fun.

"Reminds me of the time..." she started, and I took it as a cue to leave.

"Nope, not doing those stories yet, Lauren, nice try, goodbye!" I said, laughing to myself and walking away.

We left for the evening to our own homes, but when I pulled into my old homestead, I paused for a minute, thinking about my old summers at Wild Rose House. Lexi was right, we'd had bonfires at least a couple times a month in the summer, inviting neighbors and kids from school. It was a big part of my memories and I found I was happy to share that with my daughter.

But the memories were growing bigger and bigger in my mind and I could see the snowball happening as they kept building. Soon that snowball would be too large and it would knock us all over. I needed to slow it down somehow, to prepare, be ready.

Luckily Lexi was there to distract me with new memories she'd make. She talked on and on about who she'd invite and what she'd wear and what they'd need for the party. "S'mores and hotdogs of course," she said, jabbering away. Listening to her go on about what she'd write in her letter to David, I promised myself to push the snowball back as far as I could and let it slowly unravel itself as it was meant to. I would give my kid the greatest summer I could, one that would rival my own teenage summers. It was the least I could do.

Chapter 21

The night of the Wild Rose House bonfire was warm and humid, the type of Midwestern summer evening that would cool a bit when the sun went down. The corn was high and swayed with a gentle breeze. I stared out at the landscape as I helped place logs and blankets, and set out coolers and roasting sticks for hotdogs and s'mores. A shadow of memories distracted my thoughts, but I tried to stay in the moment as much as I could.

With the moon high and almost full we didn't need all the exterior lights on, but we lit all the citronella torches to help control mosquitos.

I laid down on a blanket and looked up to the wide sky at the constellations, which glowed so much brighter here than in the big cities. I took a deep breath and let the bigness of it all engulf me. I'd always loved the country sky. I'd spent so many nights lying on a blanket looking up at the stars and the moon, listening to music and thinking deep and meaningful thoughts. It healed me when I was broken, and I wasn't immune to the power of it that evening.

I wished David could be there with me, sharing the evening, talking and laughing like we used to. I missed my person. Though I'd learned to be ok living on my own, I still preferred being stuffed together in an apartment arguing over where the silverware drawer should be or who would be the one to get up and make coffee since the bed was so comfortable it was difficult to move.

"Hey Mom, did you want to be alone or would you like some company?" Lexi stood over me, bending to lie down next to me once I gestured the ok. "It's really different out here," she said. "Beautiful."

We spent a few minutes pointing out constellations and enjoying the peace. After a bit Dottie came and joined us too.

"I'm so glad you girls are here," she said quietly. "I can't begin to tell you how good this is for my psyche having my family here together. Do you mind if we just take a few more minutes to lay here before all the kids get here?"

We three quieted again, each thinking our own quiet thoughts, before needing to get up and finish the setup. I really hadn't felt as content as I did that night in a long time, with my mother and daughter in the same space, everyone getting along. It was as if a part of myself had been closed off and was slowly opening back up and I could take a full breath again. It was nice.

As Lexi's friends filtered in, I showed them all how to use the hotdog roasters and how to find their drinks and spots to sit around the fire. The teens were all well mannered and seemed to really like spending time together. Lexi had found some good friends already, and school hadn't even started yet. I was so proud of my daughter's resilience and brave spirit, so much like and unlike my own self.

Matty ran in and hugged Lexi, raising her up and causing her to squeal and giggle and playfully tell him to let her down. I raised an eyebrow in surprise, but the two were cute together. Matty seemed to care very much about Lexi and treated her with respect, something extremely important to me. I would love to see my daughter have the type of relationship I had with David, though it might be nice for her to see her significant other a little more than I saw mine.

"Jenna, hey!" Sophie hugged me, thanking me for letting them hang that evening. "My mom wanted to come too. I hope that's ok. She's just over there with Dottie discussing the clothing trends of teenagers and how we're all degenerates." She laughed and pointed to the two women, who were deep in a discussion together, nodding and giggling every once in a while.

Eventually I heard the beautiful sound of chatting and laughing along with the roar of the fire. Someone played music, a soft sound amid the rest of the noise. I hoped Lexi and Sophie were ok with their limited hearing, but I knew after 17 years they'd advocate for themselves. Our daughters wouldn't allow anything less, I thought with a smirk.

"Hey Lauren, do you remember that one night, the bonfire on my 15th birthday?" I asked my cousin with a devilish grin. "I'm surprised Dottie even allowed this night to happen after the crap we pulled that night!" We both snorted, memories bubbling up.

"I remember, and trust me, I debated this for a while, my lovelies," Dottie butted in. "I trust Lexi and Sophie to act better than you two knuckleheads did. Besides, our Lexi wouldn't do anything wrong ever, not that angel. Sophie on the other hand..." she joked, barely hiding her smile.

"Aunt Dottie!" Lauren chided, pretending to smack her aunt in the arm. "Sophie is just as angelic as her cousin and you know it! We raised these girls right, somehow. Despite our parents looking the other way every single time we were together!"

I stared, lost in thought, remembering my 15th birthday, which was so very long ago and yet so clear in my mind.

Chapter 22

1998

"You're 15 now, Jenna! Make a wish and blow out the candles!" Penny yelled, shaking my shoulders. We were all at Wild Rose House again, doing a family party before the big bonfire. Charles and Dottie were outside setting everything up, along with Dottie's sisters Bloom and Becka and their husbands, who stayed outside drinking beer and talking about sports.

I closed my eyes and thought really hard about what I should wish for. As I decided, Ty came along and blew out my candles before sticking his finger in the frosting and running outside to hide among the grownups.

"Ty..." I started, rolling my eyes. I couldn't ever get mad at him, though. I loved his spontaneous chaos and his inability to be serious about anything at all. It made me angry, but I also envied his way of seeing everything as a game or a challenge.

Penny, on the other hand, hated Ty's mischievousness. She wanted everything to go as planned, and his wildness always messed up her carefully planned schedule. Even as they aged, she still saw him as an annoying little brother type, and she couldn't understand his constant need for attention.

"Ty ruins everything!" she yelled, pouting, arms crossed and lower lip out. "I'm so tired of him. He's like a feral cat!"

That made the other girls laugh hard and everyone started meowing, running around saying things like "I'm Tyler, I'm a feral cat!"

and "I'll bite you if you don't play every game that comes into my head!"

They were rolling on the floor laughing hysterically when Ty peeked back in the door. "HEY! No fair, you're laughing without me! What's funny?" he demanded. That caused the girls to laugh harder, and they started meowing again, causing Tyler to join in, not even caring that he didn't understand the joke—that he was the joke.

"I told you he's feral!" Penny yelled, pointing and laughing, causing Ty to hiss in response.

I had calmed down and quietly watched my friends—my family—enjoying this birthday more than any other so far. Each year was my favorite, topping all the other years, for no other reason than it just being the latest one.

I gathered the excited Wild Rose Girls (and Boy) and went outside to finish helping with the bonfire setup. I'd invited some kids from school and they'd be there soon. I wanted to make sure everything was perfect. The girls hadn't made a promise not to have boyfriends this summer, and all bets were off. I was determined to find someone to spend the summer with, so I'd had Ty invite all his best and cutest and most single friends.

Even Brian would be there. We hadn't spoken in a while, but he told Ty he still liked me. I'd worn my new lip gloss and put my hair in French braids for the occasion. I wanted to catch everyone's eye this year, so I could be the one to choose the best summer boy.

Later that evening I laid back on a blanket next to Brian, staring up at the stars. He pointed out constellations, and I ignored him, thinking instead of big important thoughts, like what it would be like to drive and go to college and have a family someday.

One of my favorite things in the world was listening to music and staring at the stars of the giant night sky. I wanted to live here forever, and always have this view. It was relaxing and recharging, and I knew not to take it for granted.

"Hi Brian," Tina whispered, quietly scooting beside him on a blanket. "Can you tell me which one is the Big Dipper?"

I rolled my eyes, knowing Tina knew exactly where every constellation was, even the ones on the other side of the earth this time of year. She was excellent with everything astronomy, and usually was the one telling everyone fun facts about the sky no one asked to hear.

I didn't want to start something, so I quietly got up and went for another s'mores. Penny saw me and followed along. Ty and Lauren did the same. We always gravitated toward each other even when our friends were around. I was often the unofficial leader, paving the way for what everyone else would do or where they would go. They waited quietly for my order, knowing I'd give it even before I did.

"Ty, does Tina still have a crush on Brian?" I asked him. He nodded and waited to see where this was going. "Even though she knows he likes me?" He nodded again and rolled his eyes. I bit my lip, wondering what to do with that information.

A wide and wicked smile broke out on his face. "Let's mess with them," he suggested. "Please, can we mess with them?" Lauren looked bored, shrugging, and Penny shook her head, everyone looked at me. I pretended to think about it before shrugging like Lauren, saying, "Yeah, ok, what'd you have in mind Ty?"

We all whispered for a bit, talking out the plan, as only 15-year-olds can do, and we spread out in our various directions to enact it, with only Penny wringing her hands and biting her lip, not wanting to get in trouble or make Tina mad.

"Tina, come with me to get some hot chocolate," Lauren told her cousin, pulling her up from the blanket. Tina protested, but Ty playfully started punching Brian, who then had to defend his honor. The boys ran off wrestling around and the girls went to get hot cocoa. A few minutes later Ty came back and whispered to his sister, "Brian wants you to meet him in the corn over there. Dummy, I think he wants to kiss you. I about threw up when he told me."

Tina blushed and asked what she should do. "Uh, go find him I guess. Just don't tell me what happens. I really will barf!" he yelled and ran back away, pretending to heave.

"Ty!" she whisper yelled. "Don't leave me. I don't know what to do!"

She looked for Lauren, who had disappeared. Taking a deep breath, Tina walked slowly toward the field, trying to see where Brian might be waiting. She whispered, "Brian?" as she walked deeper. The corn wasn't high enough to completely block her view, so she felt fairly safe looking around the stalks, but it was darker the further away from the bonfire she went. "Brian!"

"Jenna?" said a voice. "Is that you?"

"Brian?"

They found each other, Tina tripping over a corn stalk, falling onto Brian.

"Oh, I thought I was meeting Jenna in here," he said, embarrassed. "Hi, Tina... do you know where your cousin is?"

Tina's cheeks burned. How had she messed this up? She was going to kill Tyler when she saw him. She knew he obviously set her up, and she was beyond embarrassed, lying on top of a boy who didn't want her, in a field of scratchy corn.

"No, it's just me..." she said quietly. They tried to stand up when there was suddenly a flash. "Is that a camera?"

"Got you!" It was Ty, snapping photos with a camera, the flash blinding them. "Whatcha doing out here in the sticks, sister? Mom's gonna be maaaaaad." He ran off with the camera, only he went further into the field, not toward the glowing fire.

Tina ran after him, yelling at him to give her the camera. Brian ran along, trying to tell them both they were going the wrong way.

After a while Tina sunk to the ground, crying in frustration. It was dark, she'd lost Ty, and she ran so far in that she didn't even know which direction she needed to go to get back to the group. She cried harder until Brian found her, putting his arm around her to console her.

"I'm sorry, Tina," he said weakly. "I think we can find our way back if we go that way," he said, looking up at the stars as if they'd lead them back out. She was too upset to move, choosing instead to just sit and keep crying. Brian sat with her, unsure what to do.

After a bit they heard yelling. Everyone called their names, looking for them through the field. Tina saw flashlights moving around her and she called out weakly. Brian's voice was stronger as he yelled, "Over here!"

Tina's mom was the one to find her, followed closely by Dottie and me.

"Come on, let's go Tina," Bloom said harshly. "We'll talk about this on the way home." She helped her daughter up and gave Brian a glare, telling him to back away from her daughter. Tina mumbled and followed her mom back to the bonfire and out to their car to go home. "TYLER, YOU TOO!" Bloom yelled, and Ty came running from wherever he'd been, mumbling that he didn't do anything, hoping not to get into too much trouble.

I looked at Dottie, who crossed her arms. "Jenna, I know I don't have to tell you what a horrible idea all this was. Everyone's cut up from the corn, half the kids are crying or scared, and all the adults are embarrassed and disappointed. I expect you to tell me what happened or I'll go ask Penny."

I made a face at my mom and told her Penny would not understand what happened, and neither did she. After staring at each other for a minute, Dottie sighed and pointed back toward home. "Go," she said. "We'll talk about it later then."

Lauren met up with me on the way back. She squeezed my hand and raised her eyebrows, wishing me luck, before running off to find her own mom.

The night had started off my best birthday yet, but had ended in confusion and embarrassment. We hadn't meant for our prank to go that far, and I was mad at Tina for being such a baby about it. I went inside and ate some cake, alone and in trouble. We'd never be allowed to have a bonfire ever again.

Chapter 23

I stared at myself in the mirror, conjuring all the mental fortitude I could muster. I freshened my makeup, fluffed my hair, and drew out a deep breath.

I'd been invited—voluntold as her military husband would have said—to dinner at the big house, and it wasn't a normal informal affair. Dottie instructed Lexi and me to dress nice, bring wine, and be ready for some "discussion". I wasn't sure what that meant but it sounded more serious than I'd like, and I was honestly a bit concerned.

"Lexi, are you about ready, love?" I called out to my daughter. Lexi entered the small bathroom in a light blue sundress, her pink hair pulled up and makeup done. She pulled at her outfit and groaned, asking why they needed to put on a show for the grandparents.

"Dottie and Charles are particular sometimes," I reasoned. "They weren't always so stuffy, but the older they get the more they feel the need to hang on to what they call their decorum."

"Young people these days," Lexi stated seriously before laughing out loud. "No one knows how to live properly anymore." She wagged a finger at me. Her face fell. "Mom, Grama is going to talk about my hair again."

We hugged and promised we'd get through the night together, and walked arm in arm across the lawn to the big house.

"We need to use the front door, babe," I reminded the teen, rolling my eyes. Lexi had her hand on the back door, which is how she always walked into Dottie's house. She scoffed, and we walked around the house. The porch decor was red, white, and blue—an Americana theme—as was Dottie's favorite summer style. Everything looked freshly cleaned and there appeared to be a new welcome mat at the door. Though maybe it had always been there, and we just hadn't used the front door in a while.

We rang the doorbell, sharing a look and a smirk. We waited a full two minutes before finally opening the door as I yelled, "Mom! I'm coming in!"

Dottie hurried toward us and told them to just wait. "I was just getting to the door, sweetheart, you don't need to yell." I opened my mouth to argue but just shut it again and nodded.

I handed her a bottle of wine instead and commented how nice the front porch looked all decorated. Dottie waved me off and shuffled into the kitchen. "It's been like that since Memorial Day, honey. You should really pay more attention to your mother, you know," she chided on her way.

Lexi and I made our way to the dining room. Sitting in the newly reupholstered chairs were Lauren and Sophie, along with Sophie's dad, Dirk. I hadn't seen the man in years, and it was awkward having him sitting there, drink in hand, like he'd been there with us all along.

As we got closer to the table he stood up and reached his hand out to me, then to Lexi, shaking and introducing himself. "Good to see you Dink," I said to him, smiling widely. Behind me Lauren choked on her drink, stifling a laugh. "It's been a while, hasn't it?"

"It's Dirk, actually," he told me, completely missing my jab. I nodded, pretending to care. I wasn't fond of him—had never been ever since he'd started dating my cousin the summer before their senior year. The couple had legally separated, not quite divorced, I'd learned recently, so I wondered why he was even there at all. I looked at Lauren with a raised eyebrow and she shook her head slightly and put her hands up as if to say she had nothing to do with it.

"I'm Lexi," my teen said quietly. "Nice to meet you, sir."

"You look like a cotton candy version of Sophie here," he told her. I could see then and there Lexi decided she didn't care for him either. She looked questioningly at Sophie, who rolled her eyes.

"Wow, thank you, Dink," she told him loudly, winking at me, and moved over to her cousin. He mumbled the correction to his name as Lexi and Sophie tuned out the grownups, hugging each other and complimenting their outfits.

They sat together and talked excitedly, each needing to resort to reading lips and texting each other to fully understand each other amid the adults beginning their accusations and questions as to why everyone was there.

"Mom, why aren't you in here explaining all this?" I yelled to the kitchen. The doorbell rang and everyone looked at each other. When it rang again, I got up and huffed in exasperation. "I'll get it, I guess?" I mumbled and went toward the entryway.

I opened the door to find Penny standing at the porch, dressed nicely but pulling at her heels, cursing as she almost lost balance and fell.

"Oh, ok, well, let's just have a freaking party why don't we," I yelled toward the kitchen, walking back toward the dining room. I left the door open, making Penny walk in and close it on her own, confused and embarrassed. "MOM! Who else should we expect tonight? Did you invite the PRESIDENT too?"

Just then the doorbell rang once more. My face must have shown all my emotions at that point—confusion, anger, overwhelm, and something akin to fear. I knew who was behind that door before it opened. Dottie had gone too far this time.

As the panic rose to the surface, I walked quickly to the hallway bathroom and entered it quietly, locking the door. I slumped to the floor and put my head into my hands. The tears wouldn't come, but the pain behind my eyes felt like it was dangerously rising to the surface. I'd specifically stayed away from Iowa for the past 20 years for this reason.

I didn't want all these people in the same room with me. And now I couldn't avoid it unless I snuck out the window like a teenager.

I opened the bathroom window and thought about it. My 40-year-old body would NOT be happy with that decision, but I could probably squeeze through. Closing the window, I sighed and sat inside the clawfoot tub like Lexi and I used to do when things got too heavy emotionally.

As if being summoned, I heard a knock on the door and a "Mom, can I come in, please?" I got out of the tub long enough to open the door for my daughter and crawled back in the tub, Lexi following me.

"We're too big for this," she said, struggling to fold her legs in, laughing at the process as she struggled to keep her dress over her knees. "Mom, I don't know what's happening. There's someone out there saying he's my cousin Tyler. I have a cousin Lauren that I've never known about until recently, and the first person I met in this weird town is also my cousin. Are we related to Penny too? Who are all these people? And why are we hiding in the bathtub?"

I stared straight ahead, processing it all.

"Ty is your cousin, Lex. That's true," I started. "There are like 9000 people in this town and we're magnets for the ones we're related to. I don't know what else to say. Dottie went too far with this stunt."

That left Lexi with way more questions than answers, but she knew to just sit quietly and let her mom process in her own way. She grasped my hand and squeezed, letting me know she's listening.

"No, we're not related to Penny. She's been my best friend since before we could walk so she's as close as anyone to family, but everyone else in there is blood."

I wrinkled my nose.

"Except for Dink."

"Uhm, it's Dirk actually," Lexi said in a mockingly gruff voice, breaking the tension. I leaned over and hugged my kid, slipping and hitting an elbow on the edge of the tub. Cursing, I said we'd better get up and go face everyone. I checked my makeup in the mirror, straightened my shoulders, and took the deep breath of faith that would hopefully get me through the rest of this night. I promised Lexi we'd continue the story later, but for now I needed her to just trust me and help me get through this with her.

Pasting on a smile, I opened the bathroom door and motioned for Lexi to go ahead. I wasn't ready to see Ty, but I had to face him, eventually. Besides, I couldn't kill my mother without seeing her.

Chapter 24

I looked around the table at everyone, no one speaking. I watched Lexi do the same, sneaking a glance at Sophie raising her eyebrows, obviously just as confused. I concentrated hard on the plate in front of me, schooling my emotions.

The table setting was beautiful, of course. Dottie was a simple woman, but she didn't like things out of place and her sense of decor was spotless. The white on white stoneware wasn't the slightest bit discolored or chipped. The polished silverware practically sparkled with the lights from the simple crystal chandelier reflecting from it.

I took a slow drink from my water glass, and Lauren cleared her throat. It was Dottie who was first to speak, taking a deep breath before welcoming everyone to dinner.

"I haven't had you all around my table in two decades," she said with a pained look on her face. The look aged her, and I saw for the first time the pain that still weighed heavily on this family I hadn't even bothered to tell my daughter about.

"I'm sorry to do this all to you," she started again. "I understand you are adults and you may do whatever you want, talk to each other or not. But Charles and I need to talk to you about something important and we need you all here. Please don't be dramatic. Please don't run away. Just listen. OK?"

She turned to look at each of her younger family members, who all nodded slightly in promise to be good. She lingered on me, giving me a look to let me know she was especially warning me not to run. I rolled my eyes as I nodded, and I couldn't help but smirk thinking back to my teenage years. Sophie noticed my face and elbowed Lexi to keep her from laughing. They both looked slightly afraid of Dottie, who cleared her throat and waited to make sure everyone was listening.

"Charles and I are fine, to start. I just wanted to say that right away, before you start stealing the silver and calling dibs on my things. But we know we're not getting any younger, and we've both had a couple of small health scares that left us questioning everything." She looked at her husband, who sat at the opposite head of the table. The two were monarchs, ruling the family that night, something they hadn't been able to do in a while.

"We're going to renew our vows—and our wills—and we want you all to be there," she continued. "Charles and I need you to get your lives together and stop whatever had kept you apart for so long. Someone is going to have to take over the farm when we go and I need you to tell me right now who I can trust with it. The lawyer needs to know which name or names to put in the will. I've tried over and over to speak with you and no one gives me the time of day anymore. You are all 'too busy' to talk about anything important."

Everyone opened their mouths and closed them again, no one daring to be the first to speak. She had put us all in our places.

Penny was the first to weigh in, saying loudly, "Dottie, I'm not even family. Why in the world am I here?" She quickly stood up, visibly annoyed. "You have always lumped me in with the other kids but I'm not related, and it's always painfully obvious that I don't belong when you start in on some family drama argument. I thank you for inviting me yet again, and I will absolutely be at your vow renewal party, but right now I'm leaving."

Dottie raised her hand, holding court. "Sit down Penelope and listen to me." Penny sat immediately, eyes wide and lips pulled tight. She huffed and crossed her arms in front of her but waited quietly.

"You are a member of this family. You aren't blood, but you've been here since the beginning along with the others, and you know it. You are in my will as much as my daughter and my nieces and nephew. My sisters Bloom and Becka have excused themselves from inheriting anything, being older than me and frankly not wanting anything I have to offer, but they asked that I care for you as they do. Ty, I was so sorry to hear about your dad's passing a few years ago, and I know your mom isn't crazy about living at the facility, but she's tough and she's doing well. She and I still keep in touch, unlike her son and me." She raised an eyebrow and Ty lowered his head.

Dang, this was getting difficult to watch.

"Lauren, it's harder to reach your mother, what with her and your father retiring to God knows where. She's living it up and leaving you to tackle life all by yourself, and I am sorry for that." Lauren nodded, looking pained. Her mother had never been motherly, which is what drew her to the Wild Rose Girls over and over. Dottie took care of them like her own mom never could. "I have grand hopes that you will help me with the planning of the ceremony, as you've always had exquisite taste."

Lauren smiled lightly, trying not to gloat.

"Dirk, I was unaware until tonight that my niece had drawn divorce papers. You are here in error, I'm afraid, so please know you may enjoy my food and wine but you will never again step foot on this property. I have never been fond of you, and now I don't have to pretend. I am an old lady and can do whatever I want."

Sophie gasped, and Lexi snorted a laugh. Dirk shuffled in his seat, nodding in acknowledgement. This dinner party was getting ruthless. I loved every minute of the drama, though I was still scared and extremely uncomfortable.

"So I ask again, my children, can I count on you to join Charles and me for our ceremony? Can we count on you to step up and care for this house when the time comes? Charles and I are so very tired of keeping up this large property. Perhaps we should retire to an island as well," she winked to Charles, and he nodded, smiling lightly. He was a man of few words, it seemed, but he was his wife's sturdy champion.

Everyone turned toward each other, Ty and I making painful eye contact before each looking at another set of green eyes. I wondered if Lexi had noted the family trait immediately as everyone gathered around the table.

"Dottie, you know I'm a realtor, and of course I'll help with the house and property if you need to sell it," Lauren finished as Ty said, "I can't do this."

Penny literally sat on her hands, not wanting to come between everyone, but obviously wanting to say something–everything.

I broke the tension, standing up. Lexi knew this move, and drew in a breath. I had thought about it all, come up with a plan, and I was ready to make the moves. It was my big moment, the one I had after every deployment or PCS move announcement. I'd stay quiet, gather my thoughts, and execute the plan.

"Lauren, we aren't selling the place. That's just not happening. Ty, you CAN do this. Penny, you're one of us." I paused and looked at each of them, taking a deep breath before going in for the kill.

"We're all in this, Mom." I paused again, waiting for each of the cousins to nod. "We're so happy for you and dad wanting to renew your vows and of course we'll do whatever it takes to give you the ceremony you deserve. We'll host it here on the property and I'm sure Lauren and Penny would be an amazing help with all those details."

I turned to smile at my mom and then my dad, making sure they understood they would all be there for them.

"Ty, please come to the party. You know you always have a place here. This was as much your home as your own when we were kids, and I'm sorry if you've felt you had to stay away on my account."

I only allowed myself a moment to feel sad before I turned to Penny and Lauren, my two Wild Rose Girls sitting on each side of me. "You're the closest thing I have to sisters, and I'm sorry I haven't shown you that in the last decade or two. I have my reasons, and I'm not about to forget about everything that's happened, but Mom's right, we need to figure something out while we have time. We're family, all of us."

To Dottie I said, "We'll do it. Anything you need. We're here for you, Mom."

Everyone started talking at once. Lexi and Sophie glanced at each other, their eyes wide. They could never hear what was being said when everyone spoke over each other. I was sure they were speaking worlds in their looks to each other. It warmed my heart to see their relationship grow, and I was about to say so when my thoughts were ripped away by a drunk idiot, who until that point had been silently nursing his wounds.

"Sure, of course you'll take the whole farm, Jenna," Dirk spewed loudly over everyone else, taking another drink of his wine. "Jenna gets everything, right? Marriage to an American hero, money, life traveling everywhere... of course you'll get the house too. You probably won't even live in it. You'll be too busy living in Japan or Hawaii to be anywhere near us little folks."

Everyone stopped talking and stared at him with wide eyes and gaping mouths. No, he didn't; I thought.

I was about to reply, when Charles stood up, his chair scraping loudly across the floor. "Get out," he said, not waiting to see what his wife wished for him to do. "Get out of our house. You are no longer welcome here and I need you to leave."

"Yeah, Dink, I think you need to go. You're an idiot. Jenna's their daughter. Of course she'll get the house she grew up in. You're out of line and you need to go home. Call a car service. You're drunk," Ty told him, giving him space to pull his chair out. He led the stumbling man to the door and locked it behind him.

"I hate that guy," he mumbled on his way back. He raised his head, startled to see the group looking at him, collectively trying not to laugh. "What?" he asked. "I really hate that guy. I'm sorry Sophie, I know he's your dad. But literally the last thing that guy told me before I slammed the door in his face is 'It's Dirk, actually.' and I just can't."

It only took a second for Sophie to laugh, and everyone else joined in. She told them it was fine. I was sure she loved him because he was her dad, but she obviously knew his downsides very well. It'd mostly been her mom and her, as her dad didn't seem to enjoy being around much. Now that we were here, I vowed we'd never let her feel alone or abandoned. She was one of us, just as we all were, and I sat there for a few minutes just taking that all in.

The rest of the night went better. We ate dinner, not talking too much, and as soon as we finished I announced I needed to go.

"I'm sorry Mom, I just need some space to think," I told her with a hug. "Ty, it was good to see you. I hope the drive wasn't too bad. Are you staying in town or heading back?" Ty said he needed to get back to Iowa City, where he lived with his roommate and a couple dogs. He apologized for not staying longer, but I waved it off, understanding completely. I wasn't the only one who needed space.

On our way out the door to head back to Wild Rose House, I noticed Dottie hugging Ty fiercely. "I wish Tina was here," she told him. I glanced at Lexi and hurried across the lawn, avoiding her gaze again.

One more secret, I thought, feeling Lexi side eye me. Just one more, and it'd likely come out soon now that everything else was in the open. I felt gutted, raw, and depleted. I wasn't sure we'd make it through the last one.

Chapter 25

I woke the next morning with a headache, and with Lexi standing beside my bed with a cup of coffee.

"Here, you'll need this," she told me as I sat up and gingerly accepted the mug from her. She sat down beside me and waited until I took a couple sips before saying anything else.

"It's time, Mom." The words I'd dreaded every day but especially since leaving Dottie's house last night. I'd gone straight to bed, promising we'd talk later. Now it was later, and I didn't even know where to start.

I groaned and kept slowly drinking my coffee, willing my brain and body to wake up and handle this correctly.

"There's a box in my closet," I told Lexi, pointing. "Will you please get it and bring it over?" She did as I asked and opened the lid, pulling out the framed photo I'd found when Dottie brought me the box.

I could see the recognition on her face as she saw a younger version of me smiling at her—one that looked so much like her own reflection. She flipped the frame over and read the names.

"Jenna, Lauren, Penny, Tina," she ran her finger over each name as she spoke it. "Mom, I heard that name last night, and it sent you into a shutdown. Please, no more secrets. No more hiding." She handed me the photo and sat down beside me on the bed. "I've learned this summer that Wild Rose House has all this history. I met my cousin! I met Penny, and Lauren, and Ty! Why haven't I met Tina? Why wasn't she at Grama Dottie's dinner?"

Tears welled up in my eyes as I thought about the summer of 1999. I nodded, letting myself picture Independence Day, ready to spill it all.

Chapter 26

1999

"Hurry up, Tina, we're gonna miss the fireworks!" Ty yelled to his sister, who was glued to the mirror, perfecting her makeup. "You look fine, let's GO!"

It was the 4th of July and I was at the twins' house for once. Dottie had dropped me off on her way out with Charles and we were due to meet our cousin and friends in a few minutes. Ty was mad; he hated when Tina made him late. He didn't want to miss a single minute of the fun and Tina loved to make a fashionably late entrance. I was used to the fighting between them, but I'd wished they'd just picked me up on the way. I never knew how to react and whose side to take when they put me in the middle of their arguments.

Finally, Tina walked out of the bathroom, smiling and giving Ty and me a little curtsey before flipping her brother off with her middle finger. "I'm ready now, your majesty, geez. Grab your shoes, loser, I'm driving." They'd gotten their licenses a couple months ago and their mom made them share a vehicle until they could afford their own. I didn't have a car yet, so I was at the mercy of my family members driving me around. Tina grabbed the keys to their beat up old truck and Ty grabbed his shoes. I ran behind them, eager to get out of their house.

We got to the park late and had to walk what felt like a mile to find our friends, who had set up blankets and a cooler ahead of time so we'd have a good spot. Every year the city hosted a fireworks show, and we gathered to watch together, this year special because most of us could drive ourselves.

"Heyyyy Jenna, Tina, Ty made it! You guys, it's almost dark! You 'bout missed the whole thing!" Brian slapped Ty a high five and gave Tina a goofy smile before looking at me. He knew she had a crush on him and he played into it a bit, even though we had been off and on for years. We were sort of off again, and I tossed my hair and winked before turning to chat with some other friends.

"Do you have someone to sit with, Brian?" Tina asked him, fluttering her eyelashes. "I'll sit with you if you're lonely." She flashed Ty a mean look as he got in her face, fluttering his eyelashes in jest. "Stop it, jerk," she told her brother before turning back to see Brian's answer.

Brian shrugged. "I was just gonna sit with Jenna, probably," he said to her. "I don't know if she'd get mad or whatever, if I sit next to you. I don't really know if we're together right now or if she is mad at me." I pretended I didn't hear the conversation, rolling my eyes to myself.

Ty told his sister to stay out of it, that it wasn't worth getting in a fight with me. "You're like sisters," he reminded her. "Brian's not even worth it."

"I heard that, dummy," Brian said and started a play fight with his friend. They hit at each other and started wrestling around the ground, laughing and calling each other names.

Tina sat down awkwardly on the blanket, embarrassed and not sure where she stood with Brian. She looked around for the rest of the group, who had spread out saying hi to everyone. An announcer over a crackling loudspeaker told everyone to find their seats because the fireworks were to start in about 5 minutes. Everyone jumped to find their spots. Penny waved and hustled over. Lauren sat off to the side with her boyfriend Dirk. They'd just started dating, and no one liked him. But the two were head over heels with each other, and they couldn't stop talking about going to college together after graduation and starting a family and buying the largest house in town. They were starting their senior year in less than 2 months. The rest of us would be juniors. The summer had flown by so fast already. The fireworks and party after was the biggest event of the summer that year and signified the halfway point; the beginning of everyone having to get ready for the next school year.

I looked over at Ty, his face scowling, annoyed at his friends coupled off and sitting together. His boys all had girlfriends now. I'd never seen him really interested in girls. He'd been on a few dates and girls were definitely interested in him. He just didn't seem to care. He always preferred to hang with us. We didn't ask anything of him. He told me once everyone else always wanted to change him, get him to dress nicer or accomplish something. He really just wanted to smoke, sneak a beer, and not think too much about anything. I didn't mind my cousin changing a bit; he was still just Ty to me. I did wish he was happier though.

"Hey Brian, I'm so glad you're here!" I decided to forgive him for whatever he did to make me mad; I couldn't remember what it was, anyway. Brian glanced over at Tina, and I could see he felt caught. I hated that. I grabbed onto his arm and he looked at me, away from Tina. We squeezed in together and waited for the show.

Brian put his arm around me and brought me in close as the first firework started. I loved fireworks. They were chaotic, but beautiful. I liked that combination and the feeling that something potentially destructive could make people happy. Maybe I'd make someone happy someday.

We all lay back, watching the flashes in the sky, listening to the booms overwhelm our ears and the crowd ahhing and cheering. The show was almost over when I heard Tina's voice.

"I can't believe you, Jenna. You treat Brian like garbage all the time and string him along, and then when he finally has enough of you and finds someone who actually likes him, you can't handle it! Let it go!"

Ty hated when his sister got dramatic, and tried to shush her before she caused trouble.

"Tina, watch the damn fireworks. Don't cause a scene," he whispered to her. He hit his friend and told him to lay off his sister. Brian shrugged and said he kind of liked her, that she was nice. I lost the ability to speak.

Tina gave Ty a look like she won and put her arm through Brian's. My mouth dropped.

"I can not believe you'd both do this to me," I said as the last firework boomed loud overheard and the crowd cheered and clapped. I wasn't even sure if I was talking to Brian or Tina. "You deserve each other." I turned and walked off, throwing myself through the crowd, Penny running after me.

Brian looked at Tina and shifted awkwardly for a moment before telling her he should go talk to me. "She deserves an explanation," I heard him yell to her over the noise. I couldn't hear what she answered as I kept walking.

Brian ran to catch up to me, grasping my arm to stop me from moving. He sent Penny back to the group so we could talk. I was hurt, and he knew it; I could see the shame all over his face. But I could also see he was about to break my heart. I'd been stupid and mean, and hadn't thought he'd actually end things. But he was choosing Tina. My breath caught in my throat as I shook my head, tears running down my face. Brian placed his hand at the back of my neck and struggled to explain something I already knew, and I suddenly couldn't let him do it. I didn't want him to speak, so I wrapped my arms around him and leaned in, touching my lips to his. He pulled me in close and it all felt ok. We'd get through this and we'd treat each other better. Our kiss was long and by that point the crowd had cleared. Everyone was watching.

Everyone including Tina. Brian slowly pulled away from me, realizing what he'd done, and turned toward Tina. We watched her face fall and turn ugly. The hope she had for her and Brian melted and she knew he'd never see her like he saw me. There was no future for Brian and Tina, not really. There never was. Her emotions went from sadness to anger and she could barely contain it.

Ty reached out to her, but she told him to back off. She said she needed to take a walk. Alone. She ran off, crying, hurting, needing space away from the scene in front of her.

We watched her run off and Ty mumbled how embarrassingly dramatic his sister was before he lit a cigarette and also went off on his own, in another direction.

I stood there, shocked, and Brian tried to comfort me. I didn't know whether to run after Tina, or Ty. I slid down to the ground, crossing my legs and letting the tears fall. Brian rubbed my back, telling me it would all be ok. He said he'd run after Ty and make sure he was ok.

I watched him catch up to Ty as he took a long drag from his cigarette. The two of them kept walking until it was too dark to see them. I looked toward the direction Tina went and I couldn't see her either. I stayed on the ground and cried. Penny sat with me, crying too. We'd never had this big of a fight. We'd never left each other like this, angry and scared, in the dark. We didn't know it was the last time we would see her alive. We shouldn't have let her go off alone. I shouldn't have.

Chapter 27

I sat back at the blankets for an hour waiting for Tina to get back. I looked at Ty, pacing back and forth, chain-smoking cigarettes and drinking the last of the beer he swiped from somewhere. Brian rubbed my back and told me she'd be back soon. Maybe we should just wait a little while longer, he told me quietly. Lauren had gone off with Dirk before any of the mess started, so she didn't know anything had happened. Penny was crying alone beside me, rocking back and forth in a ball. None of us knew what to do.

Eventually an officer on patrol asked us teens if we needed help getting home. We told him Tina had run off and asked if he could help find her. It was dark, and no one knew where she would have gone, so the officer said he'd put out a word to the rest of the officers and offered to drive us all home. We all went to Wild Rose House, where Ty called his mom. We didn't want to separate, and Tina's disappearance terrified us. We were tired from crying and knew we'd get into trouble with our parents, but we didn't know what to do. We needed them.

The rest of the night was a blur of police activity, grownups organizing search parties, teens crying, and coffee being passed around. Dottie took charge, using the house as a command center. She never left Bloom's side as she answered phone calls and updated a map with searches conducted. It was difficult for anyone to search with it being so dark, but Dottie had anyone with a truck and a spotlight out doing what they could. Some crews had to break for the night but they promised they'd start up again as soon as it was daylight. Everyone kept saying she'd surely turn up soon. "She'll come to her senses," they said. "She'll turn up soon."

Bloom forbid Ty from going out to search, as he was drunk and an emotional mess. "I can't believe the two of you are doing this to me tonight," she told him. "How will this look, Ty? Why would you do this?"

I hugged Tyler, telling him none of this was his fault. He was a good kid, and he only drank because he was waiting for his sister to get back, I said. If she'd have just come back, he wouldn't have even started drinking at all. If I'd just let Brian go, Tina wouldn't have run off in the first place. If anything, it was my fault, I told Ty, making him promise to stop blaming himself.

"The grownups keep saying she'll be back soon," I said to him. "She'll come back."

We sat in silence, listening to Penny crying. Lauren came over as soon as she heard, lipstick and hair messy. Dirk wasn't with her. He'd dropped her off and left to go out with his friends. He was one of the few people I knew that had a cell phone. She'd used it to check in when she heard the sirens. She'd had to try a few times with Dottie tying up the phone lines. She'd worried and had Dirk drive her over to see how she could help, only her boyfriend left her there and drove off. Lauren busied herself with making more coffee and thanking grownups for helping. It seemed everyone came and went, checking the map, writing notes and copying down updates, calling and yelling at the police for not doing enough.

I had fallen asleep on Ty's shoulder, and Penny and Lauren were on the floor beside us. We huddled in front of the couch, leaning against it, waiting for someone to bring Tina home so she could yell at us for giving her night the worst ever.

I woke when the sun started shining through the window. Lauren had already woken and was in the kitchen making more coffee and passing out donuts someone had brought. Dottie was awake—maybe still awake—but Bloom had passed out sleeping in the recliner. At the noise of the coffee maker beeping, she opened her eyes and jumped up from the chair, guilt on her face.

"Oh no, I fell asleep! Sis, what have you heard? The sun's up. Did they find her? Is she home?" She ran to Dottie, demanding to know everything she missed. Dottie told her not to worry about sleeping, about caring for herself. Nothing new had happened, but hopefully with the sun up they'd know something soon.

It was another hour before we got the phone call we hadn't wanted to get. Charles was on the line, crying, and I watched as my mother broke down and then gave the phone to Bloom, who screamed and dropped the phone, sinking to the ground. A police officer came to the door a few minutes later and then the whole world broke.

I tried to listen to the officer explain what happened. Everything seemed to go dark and then I was heaving, my whole body feeling like it would give out. It was my fault, I kept saying to myself. She was gone, and it was because of me. The tears burned as they fell and I felt that my head would explode if I didn't get away from all these people asking if I'm ok.

I would never be ok again.

They said they found Tina about a mile down the road from the park. She'd walked into an active construction site, closed for the holiday, and had fallen down into a pit. She was gone when they found her, nothing they could do. It had been so dark, and she'd likely died from the fall.

The police officer asked the teens for statements, and we recounted the events of the night. I wanted to tell the officer it was my fault. I shouldn't have kissed Brian right in front of her. I knew he was about to break up with me, but I just didn't want to lose him to her. It had been childish, and my choice had killed my cousin. I'd never tell a soul. I'd let it eat at me, which is what I deserved.

I just knew she'd jumped into the pit on purpose. I felt it in my bones, in my heart. I'd pushed Tina too far, and my cousin had run off alone, feeling like she couldn't live anymore. She'd done the unthinkable, and now I had to do the new unthinkable: live with it.

I imagined my cousin taking that step, rolling down into the dirt, breaking bones and hurting mentally and physically until she didn't anymore.

Tina's pain was gone, transferred to me forever. I ran to the sink and threw up, sick with anguish.

They said it was an accident. No one could have prevented it. She fell. It was so dark. Someone really should have had better signs. Someone should sue the company, or the city. Someone should pay. The rescue team got to her as fast as they could, but it was just too late. Such a tragedy. Such an awful thing to happen to such a nice family. To us.

I went to my bed in the big house and laid down, and didn't get up until my tears had dried and Dottie splashed water at my face. I didn't know how many days I'd been in bed. Sandwiches appeared on my bedside table, along with glasses of water and plates of food—casseroles brought over by everyone who knew us. I sometimes ate, sometimes sipped some liquid, but mostly just stared at the ceiling. I got up to go to the bathroom and to stretch, but otherwise I lived in bed. I lived. Tina was dead.

I didn't want to see anyone, didn't know how the others were doing, if they grieved similarly or if they made peace with the situation. I didn't care. Tina was gone. The world was broken. I was broken.

Chapter 28

"Tina died? Oh, Mom," Lexi said, hugging me tightly. "I don't know what to say. I'm so sorry. I literally can't imagine."

I nodded into her hug, understanding she was trying to picture Sophie not existing anymore, even after only knowing her a short time. I didn't want her to imagine it. I prayed she'd never experience loss like that.

"Thank you, Lexi," I whispered, pulling back a bit. "It was too painful. I don't know how I made it two more years in this town with all the ghosts of memories everywhere I turned, but after high school I left and haven't looked back. I'm so sorry I didn't just tell you. I should have." Even so, I didn't mention the guilt I felt over blaming myself, or that I feared she took her own life. There was only so much my daughter could understand. Honestly, I was a little scared of how she'd see me.

"I was so mean to her," I ventured, and then shook my head, deciding not to go there. "Anyway, Ty and Tina were twins. That day was so very difficult for all of us."

Lexi nodded, and we heard a movement in the hallway. I yelled for my mother to come in, knowing full well she'd just overheard my story.

"I'm so sorry dear, I knocked, and no one heard. I just wanted to check on you after last night. I brought coffee..." Lexi stifled a laugh as I grabbed the second cup, rolling my eyes. Everyone knew me well, it seemed.

Dottie let out a sigh and came into the room, pulling out a chair so she could face us.

"Tyler went into himself after that day," she said to Lexi, giving me a moment to drink my coffee and gather my thoughts. "He was always a spark of fun everywhere he went, but after that night he became closed off, afraid to let anyone else in. He lost his twin, his best friend, his only sibling, and he blamed himself for a long time. He had a lot of therapy, he started drinking a lot, he smoked constantly, and as soon as he graduated he left town and rarely came back. He was forever changed at 16. Stunted almost, afraid to open back up, afraid to show anyone the cracks in his heart. The poor boy."

Dottie wiped tears and took a deep breath.

"Your and Sophie's moms were never the same either," she explained sadly, sneaking a glance at me. "None of us were ok, but Lauren felt her fault in the situation was that she wasn't there that night. She'd gone out with Dink instead, which was unlike her. She always took care of her cousins, being the older one in the group. She was the big sister, and she hadn't been there."

I stood up, needing to leave the room. I said I'd be in the bathroom.

As I walked out, I saw Dottie look at Lexi gently. I shut myself in the bathroom next door and wanted to put my hands over my ears to drown out the rest of the conversation. I couldn't.

"Lexi, your mom clammed up like Ty, refused to talk about it," my mother told my kid. "I still don't know what she feels her part in the accident was, but I feel she still has something big in her heart to share when she's ready. Her trauma was unlike that of the other girls. She didn't want to talk to the officer the morning they found her. She stayed in her bed for days. I had to throw water in her face the morning of the funeral. She just wouldn't let me in. As her mother, it broke my heart. She was just a shadow of herself. Not just that summer, but until she graduated. Until she left. It was your dad who finally brought out her smile. It was that relationship that saved her. You saved her."

I stayed in the bathroom a few more minutes, bawling my eyes out. Once I'd composed myself I went back to see Lexi and Dottie had moved to the kitchen, making breakfast together. Dottie had just ended a phone call, and she immediately directed Lexi to find bowls and ingredients. Seeing me, she waved me in and put me to work, just like she used to when I was young. I smiled, thankful for the job to do, and got out eggs and bacon from the refrigerator.

We laughed as we made waffles, eggs, bacon, and used the rest of the meager selection of fruit for a giant breakfast.

I heard a knock at the door, and Dottie rushed to answer.

"That'll be your father," she told me. "If you won't come to breakfast at our house, we can certainly eat here." I'd barely spoken with my father since we'd arrived. We exchanged small talk and notes about what needed done on the house or when to come over for dinner. I found I was nervous having him in my space, among my things, even though he owned the home.

"I assume you talked about everything," he said in way of greeting. Dottie nodded, reaching to kiss her husband's cheek. "Good," he said, nodding. "It's all out. We don't have to keep secrets and pretend it didn't happen. This is good."

He grabbed a piece of bacon as we took plates to the table to eat. He took a deep breath and let it out slowly. "I was with the crew that found her," he said. This was probably the most Lexi had ever heard her grandfather speak, and I noticed how she strained to hear every word he spoke. "I watched them bring her body up, and I knew she was gone, I just knew it. The only thing I could think was how will we tell our Jenna.." his voice broke. "We didn't just lose our Tina that day. We lost our daughter too, in a way. Jenna never wanted to be here with us after that." He glanced at me and I thought again how strained and unemotional we had become as a family unit. I hated thinking they tiptoed around my feelings, thinking I'd run off again.

"Being here was painful, I think," he said to Lexi, glancing at me again as I nodded lightly. "It was painful for all of us, but she took it especially hard. They were just kids. I wish I could go back and undo that awful night for all our sakes. Tina didn't deserve what happened to her. She was so young, and such a good kid." Dottie patted his arm, and we ate in silence for a bit. For the first time in a while the silence was comforting, and I was truly happy to have my parents with me. We'd missed so many years but we had this. I smiled at each of them and thanked them, not needing to specify. My dad retreated back into his quiet ways, but when he nodded, I could see a new sense of relief behind his eyes.

Chapter 29

I listened to the chimes of the video call and waited for David's face to show up on the screen. Whenever I had a tough week, I just wanted to see my husband's face. He'd always been my rock and my constant, even when he was thousands of miles away.

"Hi, Jenna!" he said to the screen. I could see him adjusting the phone and waited for him to smile at the camera and give me a thumbs up. "I've missed you so much! I've been getting emails from our daughter... things have been tense. Talk to me, beautiful."

I blew a kiss at the screen. "I miss you, babe. It's been such a rollercoaster here. It's been such a blessing seeing Lexi and Sophie bond. It's making my heart hurt but also it's healing me a bit, day by day, seeing her connect with her family. I feel so guilty keeping them apart, not even telling her she has a cousin. David, they look so much alike. I can't believe it, the same eyes, the same facial expressions, and they both have hearing aids! I wish I had known about her years ago. I wouldn't have wanted to keep them apart, regardless of the rest of this mess..."

David shook his head and waited for me to stop rambling. He loved how much passion went into every word I spoke or wrote, and he knew sometimes he just needed to let me keep talking until I figured out what I was actually feeling. I didn't want him to tell me how I should feel, so he just listened and waited for me to ask his opinion.

"David, why do I feel so guilty?" I finally asked.

"Babe, let's just back up a minute. Look at this photo Lexi sent me." He held up a photo he'd printed of Lexi, Sophie, and their friend Emmy. "Look how beautiful our daughter is, and how incredibly happy she is!" I nodded, tearing up. "It doesn't matter now how long it took for them to meet. You did this, Jenna, you gave her this gift. I think you going back home this summer was the best thing you could have done for both you and her. I wish so bad I could be there to share it with you, but don't minimize the gift you gave yourself just because it took you a while to get there."

I smiled and asked when he'd gotten so wise. I loved running my thoughts by him and loved that he always listened before speaking. He never interrupted or made me feel less for my constant runaround thoughts. I loved that man with my entire being and I wished he could be here too.

I told him so, blinking back tears. We spoke for a while about Lexi and getting her ready for school, and about the missions he could talk about—ones that weren't classified. We laughed, cried, and when Lexi walked in the room, we all talked together and for a few moments it almost felt like David was there.

When we ended the call, I hugged Lexi and apologized for everything I'd ever hidden from her, and everything I kept her from experiencing.

"Everyone should be able to know their family, and I'm sorry, sweetheart."

"It's ok, Mom, I've had some time to think about it a bit and I'm gonna be honest, it's been a lot. Sophie didn't know any of this either. We're confused, a bit frustrated we didn't have each other when we needed each other. We both have hearing loss, Mom. It would have been seriously nice to have someone to talk to about it, because you know I have had NO ONE."

She paused and watched my face fall. I deserved that, and I bit my tongue, letting her get it all out.

"I'm not mad, Mom," she told me, trying not to pile emotion onto us both. "I was. But it's not worth being mad. You didn't even know anything about her anyway—I get it. You weren't actively keeping me from her. I have Sophie now, and I have Dottie, and Charles, and Lauren, and Penny. And I met Dink, and Ty... I would have loved to know Tina too. I'm so thankful I know these people. It sucks that I didn't know them before, but we can't go back and change things. We move on, right? Whatever happened, we move on, and we live life right now. YOU taught me that."

She leaned in and rested her head on my shoulder.

"I taught you that?" I asked my daughter, tears in my eyes. How did I get so lucky to have this girl as my kid? Lexi nodded into her hair. "Wow, I'm really smart," I joked and Lexi elbowed my side lightly.

"I love you, girl," I told my daughter. "You're growing up so well and I don't know how it happened. I'm a mess, and I've had all this trauma and hid it all for your entire life, and your dad's deployed and you have every right in the world to just be angry. How are you doing so well?"

Lexi shrugged and smiled into my hair, hugging me tight. "It's gotta be this Iowa weather," she joked. "The cornfield is magical, and the humidity is leaking into my brain."

She drew back and gave me a serious look for a moment.

"Can you tell me about Tina?" she asked me. "It's ok if you aren't ready. I just want to know how you were as a kid, as a teen. Maybe, if you want, you could tell me about your Wild Rose Girls?"

I smiled wide and told her I'd love to talk about my childhood. Now that everything was out in the open I was remembering a lot more of the happy parts, like the birthday parties I threw every year or our first school dance.

We spent the next hour talking about Penny's insecurity, Tina's jealousy, Ty's absolute chaos, and Lauren's maturity.

Lexi hung on to every word, laughing and loving hearing how everyone fought and loved so hard. She'd never had a sibling or, until now, cousins, but I painted a clear picture of how wonderful my childhood had been before the accident and it was like she saw me for the first time, as I really am.

For me it was the beginning of something new. It was healing. Sharing with Lexi right then felt like the exact right timing, and though I was still riddled with guilt, I could finally see everything would be ok.

Chapter 30

I swallowed my pride and text Penny, asking her to meet me in the newspaper office when she had time. I could feel my heart race a bit as I sent the message. I felt like I was taking a step in a direction that would change my path forever. Reaching out to the friend I'd barely spoken to for half my life wasn't as difficult as I thought it'd be, however. Seeing her a few times over the past few weeks definitely took the sting out.

I heard the door ding as Penny walked into the empty office, most likely nervously looking around the industrial space. I knew she would look at the raised ceilings, large beams and ducts everywhere, and remember the school field trip like I did walking back in after so many years. The building was one that always chose function over beauty, though there was something oddly comforting about being in a building with such a longstanding history.

Penny had always been interested in history, and in writing. Her mom didn't have much to give, but Penny spent all her free time at Wild Rose House with me or at the library reading about all sorts of topics. Her mom would often assign Penny a topic and she'd go learn as much as she could and write a report to read aloud when her mom got home from work. I guess it was her way of connecting with Penny's interests, but it also kept her focused and out of trouble.

I was in the back, so I couldn't see her look around the room with eyes that noticed details most people missed. I imagined she reached out to touch the potted plant on my desk, feeling the waxy leaves. It was fake, of course, because I have never been able to keep plants alive.

Penny laughed out loud, a sound that echoed through the expansive space.

"Penny, is that you?" I called out, having given myself a couple minutes to clear my head. I peeked my head out to ask her to wait just a minute, and Penny continued to look around the desk as she rocked back and forth on her feet. I saw her reach out again and touch a frame, one that I'm sure she hadn't seen in decades. I didn't have the heart to replace the broken frame, but she'd remember those three girls anywhere. Penny had always been jealous that she wasn't in the photo, but she always seemed so happy just to have been a part of the girls' fun. She had said so many times how she wished she'd been a cousin—a true family member. At home in her apartment with her mother she had next to nothing, but she'd always felt more comfortable being the odd one out at Wild Rose House.

I was in the backroom going through files, just trying to grab one more box, when I dropped everything, a crash echoing throughout the building.

"You good? I'm coming back, Jenna!" Penny called out, making her way through the desks toward the source of the noise. She found me still trying to grab boxes way higher than I could physically reach, and she smirked at the mess of boxes and papers that had fallen around me.

"Penny, hi," I said, out of breath. I reached my arm up to wave, letting her know I was ok. "Thank you so much for coming in. I wanted to sit out there and chat, but I'm not sure I can move out of here yet, so do you mind just sort of talking while I dig myself out?"

I sat down in the middle of a semicircle of papers and folders, old files from before everything became digitized. Penny nodded and tiptoed through the fallen boxes, carefully sorting the papers into piles as she waited for me to tell her why she was there.

"Do you remember those reports you used to make for your mom?" I asked, smiling as if I hadn't just made the greatest mess around me. Penny mentioned that she'd just been thinking about that a few minutes ago too. "You always wrote them just for fun," I continued. "I couldn't believe you didn't join the newspaper or do something with writing after high school."

Penny shrugged. She hadn't had the luxury of being able to join after-school activities—she'd needed to work to help her mom pay for their bills. Once she graduated high school, she knew she couldn't afford college, so she got a job at an office, where she stayed for a while until the coffee shop needed a manager. Lexi told me Penny had been at that cafe for a decade, that though she hated the hours and standing on her feet all day, she enjoyed the customers and her ability to be creative with the menu and advertising and helping the community. She was proud of her work, Lexi had noted, but she had a feeling Penny had been looking for a job with better hours and pay for a while. She'd seen the random job listings circled in the breakroom.

Penny kept sorting, glancing at the notes in order to place them in the right piles. She got lost in it for a minute before I threw an eraser at her, hitting her in the shoulder.

"Penny!" She looked up swiftly to see me staring at her with my hands out, sighing in exasperation. "Do you want a job or not?"

She looked at me in confusion. "What? You're offering me a job? Here? But... why?" Lexi told me more than once how Penny wanted to reconnect with me, but the past couple months had been confusing and heartbreaking for both of us as we sorted through family trauma like junk at a garage sale.

Still, I saw her face shift from confusion to intrigue. She really wanted the job. And I really wanted her to accept it.

"I need a writer, Penny. Not just any writer—I need YOU. You've always loved this town, and you've always had such a heart for preserving its charm. You are a wonderful wordsmith and I just really need you here. I want you here. If you want to be here..." I stopped rambling and looked hopefully at my friend. "Please, Pen?"

Penny shrugged, trying to play like she didn't know what she'd say for a minute, and then broke out into a grin, jumping up and down, almost sliding on a pile of papers. She quickly righted herself and narrowed her eyes at me.

"Jenna, I hope you know what you're doing, because I have no experience in this space, and I'm 40 years old. This just sounds ridiculous." She hesitated, and I gestured for her to answer the question. "Well, yeah, I'll come to work here! I'd absolutely love it! Are you sure you want me around all the time? Won't you feel, I don't know how you said it, triggered, to see me every day?"

I winced and apologized, attempting to explain how everything changed the past few days with Lexi finding everything out, but I stopped when I saw a file in Penny's hand.

"Wait, let me see that one. What are the odds..." I reached and took hold of the file, labeled "City construction June/July 1999: Possible Scandal."

"Oh my God, Jenna, is that what I think it is?"

I quickly scanned the file, filling Penny in on its contents. "According to this, the city knew there was an issue with the construction site that summer. There weren't enough signs, and there weren't enough lights. They'd gotten a dozen complaints, but they wouldn't do anything about it... The journalist compiled this file because he wanted to write a huge expose after a girl fell into the pit and died. Penny, there are notes about Tina in here, and an autopsy report!"

I slunk down to the ground and Penny made her way through the mess to sit with me. "Keep going, Jenna, what's it say?"

"So the news reported the accident but left out anything having to do with the city's fault. The editor killed the story, because the mayor and city council didn't want a scandal. This says they let people wonder if Tina had jumped—had committed suicide—because they didn't want anyone to look any further into things. The autopsy shows lots of stumbling, contusions and breaks consistent with falling, and

WOAH, get this, the security footage showed her scared and unaware the pit existed until it was too late. Someone destroyed the footage and took down the camera to avoid any speculation. Penny, is all this real? Do you think it's true? Why would they hide it like that, and why am I finding it now like a needle in a haystack of files?"

Penny hugged me from the side and told me it was fate we found this particular file on this particular day.

"But friend, we knew it was an accident, didn't we?" Penny asked. I let out a breath I didn't know I was holding and cried, huge gasps of relief, as I reached out to Penny for comfort.

"Penny, oh my God, all this time... I thought she jumped." My voice broke as I whispered through my tears. "I thought she saw me with Brian and ran off. I thought it was too much, that I'd driven her to..."

Penny's eyes got wide. "You thought she killed herself? This whole time, all these years, when you shut yourself out and wouldn't talk to any of us about any of it, you thought you were guilty, that she did it on purpose?"

She hugged me hard then, arms all the way around my crying body.

"I wish you'd said something a million years ago, Jen. I can't believe you carried that all by yourself. Listen, she didn't do it. It was an accident. The city covered it up, and they shouldn't have. We can do something about that now, though, right? Should we?"

I shook her head. "We don't need to, Pen. I know now. Oh, wow, I'm so sorry I pushed you all away. I'm so embarrassed. I couldn't deal with my own pain, my own guilt, and I let it ruin everything." I hung my head, my face red with shame and shock and a whole host of emotions running around me all at once.

I suddenly felt different about everything, and had the sudden urge to run away again out of pure self preservation. I slumped into my friend, choosing to go against my screaming mind.

"But we're here now, and we're ok, right?" I asked her, tears still streaming down my cheeks. "Please forgive me for leaving. Wow, I'm the worst."

Penny was quiet for a few minutes, stroking her hand over my hair as I let it all out. We sat in the back room for a while, crying, hugging, talking about life and all the things we'd missed when I left. The healing that had started when I arrived was just about stitched up with the news of Tina's accident report. I felt my broken heart mend in a way that could only happen with family holding the thread.

Chapter 31

1999

I felt like death itself had crawled into my body and unpacked for a long stay. I'd been in bed for days, ever since my world cracked open and everything broke apart. When my mom came into my room, pulled the curtains wide open, and literally threw water into my face, I sat up, shocked and suddenly slapped with reality.

It was the day of the funeral.

There was no way out of that one. I had to go. Everyone needed me to be there, to complete the journey of the Wild Rose Girls for the last time—to show how much Tina had meant to us all. We owed her that.

I sighed and nodded my heavy head, promising Dottie I would shower and get dressed. My mother helped me up and pushed me to the bathroom. When I was clean and feeling just a little more alive, I pulled on the dress Dottie had laid out on the bed and let her help me with my hair. Everything hurt and my heart was too broken to care if my hair was styled or not, but if it was important to my mother, I'd allow it. I honestly didn't have the energy to fight it. I was in robot mode, mimicking her motions and following whatever she directed me to do.

My mother helped me with my makeup as well and squeezed my hand when it was time to go to the funeral home. I stood in front of the mirror, noticing my brown hair braided and pinned up, small curls escaping in the front. Dottie had done a beautiful job, even though the locks lacked their usual shine and softness. My green eyes, though sunken and lined with dark circles, still shone bright against the mascara Dottie had expertly brushed on my already long eyelashes. My skin was dull, but the blush helped. I apparently passed Dottie's inspection, and that's all I could ask for. I pulled at the black dress, which went just above my knees and puffed out at the waist. I didn't know where the dress had come from, as I'd never seen it before, but I was happy to have had the outfit chosen for me. The heeled shoes, however, would not work. I stepped out of the black pumps and slid on my pink Chucks, feeling more like myself. Tina would have laughed at me wearing heels, clunking around like a newborn giraffe.

Tina would never wear shoes again, I thought, at least not in this life. My mind went blank as I allowed myself to be shuffled into the car and out again into the funeral home. The family had benches at the front, blocked off and waiting for us to sit. I barely noticed anyone else but felt Lauren squeezing my hand and Penny crying into me as she hugged me tightly. I had no more tears. They had all turned to dust, along with my emotions. I couldn't feel anything anymore, it was all numb.

The funeral went on, I assumed, and I hoped I said and did all the right things. I followed the lines and smiled weakly as people told me how sorry they were, how much they'd miss her.

They didn't even know Tina, I thought. They said they'd miss her, but they'd forget about her in a few months. They wouldn't have to live every day feeling like a part of their body was gone. I knew only a few people would really know how I felt—Ty, Lauren, and Penny. If I'd just let them, they'd grieve with me, as they grieved together. But I pulled myself away, not allowing them to comfort me. I felt I didn't deserve the comfort. I needed to go through it alone the way I made Tina die alone. It was only fair.

So I sat alone once everyone but my family left. I nodded or shook my head when someone asked a question and I took the plate of food offered to me, picking casserole pieces apart in an effort to look like I was eating. After a while Dottie collected me and shuffled me back to the car, back to the house, and to the couch.

"You don't need to go to your room just yet, sweetie. Stay out here with us for a little while and let's talk about the rest of the summer. You were going to start your job at the coffee shop, remember? When are you supposed to work, love? I'll drive you, you just need to let me help you."

Dottie spent the next few weeks helping me get up and get to work. We went back-to-school shopping. We watched movies and talked about books we read. Little by little I seemed to the rest of the world to feel better, almost back to normal. I played the part of the 16-year-old, but I continued to keep to myself. I didn't ask my cousins to come over; I ignored Penny's calls, and I refused to see Brian. As far as I was concerned Brian was just as guilty as I was, and he didn't even seem to know it. He'd moved on like it'd never happened, asking me out on dates and calling daily to talk to me. Dottie eventually told him he'd better just give me space and to please stop calling. She grew tired of relaying messages. He started dating someone else within the week.

When school started, I put all my effort into my studies, which felt safe. I neglected all social calls and didn't join a single after-school club. I spent my junior year getting grades good enough to apply to colleges far away. My goal became clear: I needed to get out of Iowa.

Chapter 32

It was going to be an awkward day, I thought silently, and there was just no way around it. The summer was ending soon, Lexi would start school, schedules would get busy—now was the time.

"Well, 20 years ago would have been a great freaking time," I mumbled to myself. "But this will have to do." I checked the placement of the couch pillows and the food, and made sure there were cold drinks in the fridge. Everything looked comfortable and inviting, which was my first goal for the afternoon. I desperately wanted everyone to know they were welcome, that this was an olive branch, not a trap.

"Lexi, how's the playlist going?" I called out to my helpful daughter, who was scrolling through her phone quietly.

"Mom, it's literally a Spotify playlist and I just need to bluetooth it to the speaker and hit play. I think I can handle it," she told me with an eye roll. She approached me with an open face and placed her hands on my shoulders, telling me everything would be fine. We were the same height. When did that happen?

"Calm your butt," she told me, the ever anxious Millennial. "I set up your 90s playlist, the food is ready, the couches and chairs are comfortable, and you are going to be great."

We breathed in and out on Lexi's count as the doorbell rang. I knew it would be Penny before I touched the handle. I pulled the door open to find my friend and new coworker squealing with her arms out, reaching for a hug.

"I'm so glad we're doing this," she squealed. "Overdue or not, this is it, babe. This is healing." She released me to pick up a small bag from the ground. "This is for you."

I carefully peeked in the bag and laughed as I pulled out a digital camera. "Wow, Pen, thank you! And this time we get you in the photo, ok?" We asked Lexi to take the first picture of us to make sure the camera worked. Penny had been my real and true best friend for almost 40 years and I had missed too much already. I wanted the only sister I'd ever known to be beside me and I was ready to make amends, starting with treating Penny way better than I had been.

We grabbed a drink and some snacks and settled in on the couch waiting for the rest of the group to show up. Lexi turned on the music and we laughed about the 90s style for a few minutes until the door opened and Lauren and Sophie yelled they were coming in and the party could start.

I met my cousin in the kitchen and squeezed her hands before pulling her in for a hug. "Thank you for coming, Laur, and for bringing Sophie too. This wouldn't feel right without the next generation of Wild Rose Girls." Sophie dropped off a box on the counter and I raised an eyebrow in question.

"We missed your birthday," Lauren shrugged. "It's no big deal, you don't have to open it," she said, pulling the box toward her. I scoffed and quickly grabbed the package from her. Laughing, I tore off the wrapping paper. Inside the box was a beautiful photo album, empty apart from one photo—one that brought tears to my eyes but a smile to my heart.

"I love this photo," I whispered, touching the printing of all 5 of us. We must have been around 9 years old, I thought. Ty and Tina were holding their fingers up in bunny ears behind the heads of Lauren and Penny, as I doubled over laughing at the nonsense. It was an awful photo, with none of us looking at the camera, but it was perfect.

"Thank you Lauren," I said to my cousin. "Now I can fill the rest with new memories, I hope." I looked up to see a nod and two green eyes wetting with tears of their own. "I miss her, every day, but something feels new, different. I don't know, I'm just at peace I guess."

Before we could turn into a blubbering mess, there was a bang on the door in a pattern that everyone knew was Ty. We girls squealed again as he waited for us to open the door and pull him inside.

A shy look on his face, he asked if it was ok he came, even though we had specifically invited him. We all stared at him with dramatic eye rolling, Lauren even committing hard to the bit, pushing him back and telling him to get out.

"No stinky boys allowed!" she whined to him as Penny laughed.

Lexi and Sophie stood back watching the scene, and I knew it'd been so long since she'd seen me act so immature and let loose like that. They laughed and snapped photos with the digital camera and their phones every so often, mindful of creating new memories.

After our performance with Ty, pushing him out the door, he jumped out of our way and ran inside, throwing himself onto the couch like he used to when we were kids.

"Ugh, I'm 40 now," he said, groaning as he grabbed his hip in jest. "I just can't do that like I used to. When did we get old?"

The day went on fairly well. I got my big apology out of the way early and everyone told me they'd get over the hurt eventually but right then they just were just happy to have their cousin back.

Sophie asked to hear stories about her mom as a child and she and Lexi laughed hysterically at the thought of us perming our bangs and going through our eras of boy bands and grunge.

It was a restorative day for the Wild Rose Girls (and Boy). Lauren and I even surprised Lexi and Sophie with a knighting ceremony of sorts, asking them to promise to carry on the tradition of Wild Rose House and honor it with laughter and love.

"We promise," the girls said, saluting. I held an ice cream scoop, tapping each of their shoulders in turn.

We celebrated with a dance party, pizza, and a late-night movie and sleepover. The moms and Penny took the beds—Lauren said our backs were not young enough for the floor anymore—and Ty slept on the couch. Lexi and Sophie had sleeping bags on the floor and they spent an hour texting each other after the adults fell asleep.

It was a perfect night, one we all hoped we could repeat. We knew we'd have to talk about serious topics later but for that night all was forgiven. For the first time in a while, Wild Rose House was content.

Chapter 33

2000

The summer before my senior year, I spent every minute thinking about my plan to get out of Willow. I worked every shift at the coffee shop they'd give me, even the ones with Penny, where I'd have to smile and pretend to be happy to earn more tips. I sent in countless college and scholarship applications–anything to avoid feeling. Disassociation felt safer than letting anyone else in, but I knew my limits.

I was kind to the customers and knew when to smile. I wore my mask expertly. But I wouldn't answer questions about what I felt and wouldn't volunteer any information about how my family was doing after the trauma of the accident. While I was cordial, I refused to talk about it and eventually everyone realized it and pretty well left me alone.

I was lonely, but I also enjoyed being alone. I felt everything and nothing, and I began writing—journaling and poetry—to help me sort through the intense emotions and emptiness.

That summer was the year I embraced writing for the powerful tool it could be. Writing allowed me to work through some of my guilt and gave me purpose. I filled notebooks with my stream-of-consciousness prose, poems, and short stories.

I hoped someday I'd get paid for my words. Maybe I'd choose creative writing or journalism for my college major and I'd be able to travel the world doing something I loved.

By the time school started again I still wasn't talking to my old friends, but I could function in class and I joined the school newspaper to boost my extracurriculars. Instantly I fell in love with the process of asking questions, researching, piecing together sources and quotes, and completing a story that readers would find interesting or educational. I broke a story about drugs in the basketball locker room. I covered the Homecoming celebrations, which made sense because I didn't want to go to the dance or football game with anyone, anyway. I wrote about the cafeteria adding more nutritious options to the menu. It didn't matter the topic; I put everything I had into it.

The newspaper saved me. It gave me that spark back after I thought I'd lost it forever.

I found I could be polite to Penny, who seemed to be everywhere, without hurting too much, as long as I continued to avoid her socially. Penny worked at the cafe and shared so many classes with me. She would have joined the newspaper staff, but she had to help her mom at home. Penny knew I was still hurting but didn't have the heart to ask why I was continuing to avoid her outside of school and work. She kept asking me to hang out, and I kept telling her no. I was kind enough to her when we were together but I secretly missed being able to share secrets and I really missed the Wild Rose House. I hadn't set foot in the house since the time of the accident, and I found I wasn't eager to, no matter how much I missed it.

The last time we'd all been there together was the day they'd found Tina's body. It was a memory Penny had probably hoped to replace with invitations to end-of-summer bonfires and girls-only sleepovers. It was a memory I couldn't seem to replace. Sometimes I wondered if we'd ever be together at Wild Rose House ever again. I wondered if we'd all ever be in the same room again.

Chapter 34

Lexi was nervous going into the last week of summer and her first day of school at Willow High. I could sense it in everything she did, her nerves on display like a new hairstyle. Her senior year was about to start and she had no idea what it would be like, if she was too far behind on college applications, if she had enough extracurriculars, if we could even afford to help send her somewhere.

With everything that had happened the past few months we hadn't talked about the future, and now Lexi had one week of summer left and no plan. I went to work as usual that morning, but college applications and testing and scholarships had been on my mind since I'd gotten out of bed. Lexi had been asleep when I left, but she text me at work asking when I'd be home. I knew immediately she'd been deep in the thought tornado as well.

I went home for lunch, walking in the door just as Lexi finished up another email to her father. Colored papers and pens were spread out on the counter all around her, with various notes and scribbles. Like me, Lexi loved lists, and planners, and sticky notes, and colored ink pens. They helped us both stay on track and keep our thoughts organized when our minds were full of chaos. She'd just finished a list and was starting her college search on her laptop when I walked in the door.

"Lexi, hi! I'm home for lunch. Let me grab a sandwich or something and we'll go through your list. I know you have one," I said with a wink. I went to the kitchen and put together a quick lunch for both of us. I handed her a plate and motioned for Lexi to start while I took a bite.

"OK, so basically I'm confused what I'm supposed to be doing and how this whole year is supposed to go, Mom. We've barely talked about MY future, OUR future, and I'm starting my senior year in a week. It's always about Dad's job and where we're moving next. Then this whole summer has been one thing after another. I'm freaking out a little," Lexi squeaked out anxiously. She handed me the list and told me they had so much to catch up on.

I scanned the list for a moment and smiled, reaching out to rub her back. "Lex, please don't stress; we can fix this easily, starting right now. OK, number one, Starting School." We made another list of all the supplies they still needed to get and where to shop for clothes and shoes. She would start the first day with everything she needed, I promised.

Moving on to number two, I pulled a stack of papers from my workbag. I'd been thinking about colleges that morning too, I told her, and I'd printed a few things to help before I'd come home. Lexi rolled her eyes and nodded, not surprised we'd had similar thoughts.

"I have the few scholarship applications I could find that I thought you'd qualify for, and that we hadn't missed the deadline on, honestly," I told her. "And your extracurriculars are fine, love. We've moved around a lot but you've always found your place, even temporarily. Any essay you write, you'll nail it, I promise. You're such a great writer." We promised to fill out the forms together and keep searching. "And Penny is a wiz at research. I'll get her on it and we'll get you your money."

I could see Lexi visibly release her stress. I was so glad we hadn't waited any longer to have this conversation. I was also hoping Penny really wouldn't mind helping. I wasn't lying when I mentioned Penny being great at research. She'd been so helpful to me at the newspaper, and I was sure she would love helping Lexi with this little side quest.

I took a deep breath for the next part of the conversation. We hadn't talked at all about what to do when the year was over. We were only a quarter of the way there, which seemed ridiculous, as so much had happened in a few months. But it was something that we needed to discuss. I was tired of having assumptions and thoughts in my head without putting them out there for everyone else to share. I'd thought a lot about this and had discussed it in great length with David the past week, but I was nervous to voice my thoughts aloud.

"Lexi, I think we need to stay here permanently," I said, closing my eyes and scrunching up my face, scared my daughter would blow up about not returning to San Antonio. I remembered the drive along I-35 and Lexi's angsty teenage attitude, staring out the window refusing to talk about leaving all her friends and starting new in the worst time to be new. I opened one eye to peek and saw Lexi grinning. The pink-haired teen rushed to hug me, putting my fears at ease.

"Mom, that makes me so happy," she said in excitement. "Like, honestly, you have no idea. Sophie is going to freak. I never thought we'd be so happy to stay somewhere." I agreed, my shoulders relaxing, and hoped we could work things out to keep the promise.

We talked for a while about our lives in Iowa and how it was an unexpected feeling of home. We discussed the state colleges, the smaller privates schools nearby, and talked about different programs at each.

"This may seem weird, Mom, but I think I want to be a writer. You know with my hearing loss written words have meant so much to me and I have always loved doing those letters to Dad..." She paused, seeing tears in my eyes. "I mean, I don't want to copy you or anything, but your job has always seemed so cool, but I was just too much of an angsty brat to tell you. Do you think you could help me figure out what I should do?"

I clapped my hands and squealed. "Lexi that is fabulous! Yes, let's talk about all the different ways you can use writing!" I gushed, feeling the excitement at my special interest about to burst. I forced myself to tone it down a little as we talked more about different degrees required for different jobs. We would do so much internet searching for colleges nearby and far away with writing programs. I would support her daughter's choice to go anywhere in the world, or even to skip college altogether and just start working. As far as I was concerned, Lexi could do anything, and I'd back her with everything I had.

I felt a strange tug on my heart. I'd spent my senior year trying to figure out how to get away from Willow, and we were now spending Lexi's senior year figuring out how to stay. David's job would be an issue. Lexi going to college would be an issue. But I loved my job at the newspaper and even loved our small home. I couldn't imagine spending the rest of my life anywhere else. I'd worked so hard to leave, but now it was time to work even harder to stay.

Chapter 35

2001

The morning of high school graduation, I still wasn't sure if I was going to go or not. It felt odd to be the valedictorian of my class while not caring about high school at all. I was supposed to give my speech about overcoming adversity and banding together as a class to do this awesome thing—graduate after all these years of pop quizzes, semester exams, late nights studying. We'd been to football championships and chess tournaments. We'd fallen in love and made lifelong friends.

At least that's what I was supposed to say. In truth, I lost my boyfriend and my cousin all at once. I lost my family and my security. I failed high school, even though I was the top of my class academically.

Dottie knocked on my door lightly, asking if I was awake and getting dressed. I called out that I was both awake and dressed, but I wasn't sure if I was going or not. I had 30 minutes to decide, so I focused on getting my makeup and hair done. Dottie opened the door a little, peeking her head in.

"Jenna, you've worked hard for this. I've seen your speech, and it's good. You can do this. But honestly, if you don't want to speak, don't. You can sit there and let someone else do the commencement speech and you can just walk the stage like everyone else. But you get one chance at this, love, and I think you need to take part. No regrets."

I looked at my reflection in the mirror, finishing curling my hair. I noticed how brown my hair was; it used to be blonder. As I aged, my hair turned darker, making it harder for me to recognize myself. My eyes were as green as ever, as I lightened the usually dark makeup for the day. Maybe I was ready for reinvention again, I thought.

Once I was ready, made over in soft colors and wavy curls, I told my mom I would go. Grabbing my purse and my speech, I walked slowly to the car, Dottie ruling that I would ride with Charles and her so I couldn't back out and embarrass them. I slumped in the backseat, scowling, and focused on my Converse shoes until we reached the Willow High parking lot. No, I still wouldn't wear heels. Seeing everyone walking into the school in their dresses, skirts, suits, and button-down shirts, I straightened my spine and took a deep breath. I let my mom place her arm around me as we walked into the school, holding my cap and gown.

Dottie squeezed my hand and dropped me at the room designated for the senior class to wait anxiously. Dottie and Charles went to the auditorium to find seats next to her sisters Bloom and Becka. Lauren had graduated the year before and went off to college somewhere in Nebraska. She hadn't made the trip—something about final exams—but her mom was there to support Ty and me.

I stood at the wall, having already gotten my cap and gown on properly. Penny made eye contact across the room and gave me a little wave, waiting to see if I'd call her over. I did not. I turned and looked at the rest of my classmates, feeling the nervous excitement around me. Taking it all in, I found I really wanted Tina and Ty to jump into my field of vision, demanding attention and making me laugh. Instead, Ty stood a few feet away, also slumped against the wall, looking as uncomfortable as I felt. Everything was still wrong, even almost two years later.

I nodded to Ty, and he rolled his eyes, making me smirk and roll my eyes in return. I shouldn't have shut Ty out; I knew he needed someone after his sister died. But I also knew he looked at me the way I looked at him—a painful reminder that life was unfair and it was bound to stay that way.

Eventually the class mom clapped her hands to get everyone's attention and had us form a line to go to the auditorium for the ceremony to begin. They would hear from the principal, the class president, and then I would give my speech. After that we'd all walk the stage and receive our diplomas. Easy peasy.

I stayed in my line and sat in my assigned chair, facing the stage. I listened to the principal talk about how lovely the class of '01 was, how driven and strong we were. He spoke to the parents, thanking them for their dedication in helping their students succeed. He thanked local businesses and the staff at the school. Then he addressed the students themselves, telling them to choose their paths wisely, using what they'd learned at Willow High, blah blah blah. I was losing interest quickly. I clapped when everyone else clapped and then listened to the class president's speech about maximizing fun in life.

Suddenly it was my turn to address the crowd and my fellow students. I stood up and turned to look around the auditorium. My family clapped, cheering at hearing my name. My classmates gave me mixed reactions, some jealous that I was the number one student, others with a look of pity—one they'd given me for the past two years. I was the girl who didn't care about anything but her grades, the girl who used to host legendary bonfires but now slinked away from everyone and wore too much eye makeup. Once there were stories of me getting bit by snakes in the cornfield, and now there weren't any stories at all. I was a ghost roaming the high school hallways and barely taking up space in class. Penny gave me a smile and a thumbs up and Ty shrugged his shoulders, giving me the look I'd been waiting to see, the one that told me none of this mattered.

I nodded my head slightly and winked at my cousin and walked toward the stage. I held my shoulders back and my head high. I walked one foot in front of the other, set on a path. I walked up to the stairs that would take me to the podium where I'd give my speech and everyone would clap for me, happy to see the sad girl looking more adjusted and ok again.

I only hesitated for a second before turning and walking away from the stage, one Converse sneaker in front of the other, out of the auditorium and straight toward the entrance of the school. I heard the gasps behind me as I picked up my pace, running, throwing my cap and gown behind me. I felt free as I tore my shoes off and ran along the grass barefoot, whispering, "Tina, this is for you."

Chapter 36

Saturday morning, the weekend before school started, Lexi woke me up early, literally jumping on my bed like she used to when she was a toddler.

"Mom, come on, get up, it's morning," she said, shaking me into awareness. "The sun's up, school starts Monday, and we need to get going! Shopping Day, MOM!"

I smiled and popped an eye open. I loved when Lexi got excited about something. She would feel it in every fiber of her being, and it would glow around her, infecting everyone who saw her.

"Five more minutes," I groaned, knowing Lexi would never allow it. She'd already gotten dressed and her hair was curled. "Lexi... are you wearing makeup?"

"YES, now come on! Go get in the shower. We'll get coffee at The Cup before we get going." I sat up and gave a small salute, recognizing her marching orders. Lexi pulled my arms, helping me get up and going. I was lucky I could blink a few times and wake up quickly, after years of living with David's odd schedules, because my daughter was not allowing for any slowness. I showered and dried my hair, putting on the outfit Lexi laid out for me on the bed.

"Why do you want me to wear a DRESS, Lex?" I called out as I pulled on low-heeled shoes. I walked a couple steps in them and kicked them off, putting on my Chucks instead. I walked out of my bedroom to find Lexi had done the same. I winked and pointed a toe toward her. "You can make me wear a dress, but I'm not doing heels, my friend."

Lexi just shrugged and smiled. We had that in common, along with so much else. We quickly finished getting ready together and headed into town.

We got coffee and a pastry at the cafe, which was oddly empty for a Saturday morning. Penny stopped us and asked if I could help her with one quick thing at the newspaper before we left. It was important, and needed to be dealt with before print, she said. I looked at Lexi, who shrugged and said, "Better deal with it now. I'll come along, it's fine."

We walked down to the news office and Penny unlocked the door, holding it open for us to walk inside. I was all business, asking my coworker to tell me exactly what the problem was so we could work it out together. I was mid-sentence when I heard a "Surprise!" and looked around to see dozens of people standing in the now crowded office.

I wore a shocked look on my face as I took in the sight. Penny grabbed my hand and explained that everyone wanted to thank me for my part in saving the newspaper and restoring the town. I waved a hand in front of me in protest, stating that I hadn't done anything, all while tearing up.

"You did everything," the former news editor-in-chief said from behind me. "You came back after being gone a couple decades and jumped right in with everything you had. I was ready to fold, after losing all my employees and being unable to balance the budget. I was done. And then you came back into town full of fire and I knew we were going to be okay. YOU did that. Thank you, Jenna."

I was so touched. I thanked everyone and asked why they were hiding in the office. Penny told me they were to keep me there for another couple minutes and then we were to all go to the courthouse lawn where the real party would begin. I hit my friend lightly on the shoulder, asking how in the world she could keep a secret.

"Little Penny Pen keeping something from me?" I said to her, pulling her into a hug. I could feel the eye roll and sigh as she hugged me back.

We all walked over to the grassy courthouse lawn. The decorations were beautiful, with twinkle lights and streamers and flowers all over the place. Tables of food sat randomly throughout the area and it looked like half the town was present.

"Lexi, please tell me this isn't all for me," I whispered to my daughter. Lexi shrugged.

"I mean, it kind of is, Mom. The people here like you."

Lauren and Sophie found us then, reaching to hold my coffee and handing me a small shot of something in replacement.

"Here, Jenna, you'll need this instead," she said with a wink. I took a sip and hollered. I took another drink as we all heard the PA system whine and a loud voice ask for me to please join them at the front stage. I looked quickly from Lauren to Penny and mouthed, "no..." Lauren nodded with a smile and I finished my drink in a large gulp.

I walked toward the stage and had an urge to run away. This time though, I walked straight toward the microphone, taking it from the person who had called me up.

"Thank you for coming, everyone! I had no idea ya'll could organize like a bunch of military wives!" I paused for laughter and cleared my throat, suddenly nervous. "Listen, I was just thinking about the time I was valedictorian my senior year and at graduation I ran off right before my speech. I just.. RAN. Literally." I paused to look at Lexi, her jaw dropping at yet another glimpse into who her mother was before.

"I just couldn't face everyone. I'd focused so hard on being the top of the class but I'd let myself and everyone else down by shutting myself off. I stopped being a part of the community, and honestly I've been running ever since. I went to college in Texas, where I met my amazing husband. He was a big dreamer, and I was craving adventure, so we made a life of running. We chased the next base, the next rank, the next challenge. We carved out space everywhere we went and I was fortunate to keep working everywhere we landed."

I paused again, my voice cracking.

"But it wasn't until he deployed for a year that I could truly find myself again, in a small town in Iowa where the cornfields are big and the people's hearts are bigger."

The cheers from the audience helped me know I was right to trust the town to forgive me. I was truly among friends.

"We drove here with an SUV full of stuff," I continued. "We healed some old wounds, made some new friends and connected with old ones, and we dug back into the community that tried to help me all those years ago when I pushed everyone away. When my cousin Tina died it took something from me and I thought I needed to run away from everything that reminded me of her. But honestly, being here this year, watching you all take me back in, watching you take my daughter in, it's been the most healing thing for us both. Thank you Willow! And thank you for helping me SAVE THIS NEWSPAPER! Now go eat, drink, and be awesome!"

I took a small curtsey and winked at Lexi, who had been watching from the front. When I approached my daughter, I linked arms with her and laid my head against hers.

"I don't know how you did it, kiddo," I started. "I don't know who's idea this was or how it happened. But thank you. I wish your dad was here with us."

He couldn't be, of course, but someone had videoed the speech so we could send it to him. I cringed at the thought of my words being immortalized in video, but I was proud of my hard work and loved being able to share it with David.

We spent the rest of the morning into the early afternoon downtown with everyone, celebrating saving the newspaper and the end of summer.

"Remember all the end of summer parties we used to have?" Penny asked, eating a slice of pizza. "Bonfires, movie nights, whatever we wanted to do. Dottie was always in for all of it. This feels like a grownup version, don't you think?"

"I agree," I said, grabbing my slice of pizza. "We're never too old for pizza and a party!" I waved to some townspeople I knew and thought about my life leading up to that point. For as many tragedies as I'd had, I'd had way more blessings. I was grateful the surrounding people kept finding ways of reminding me of them.

Chapter 37

The morning of the first day of Lexi's senior year, she sprung out of bed, ready to start the day. I had woken early, shuffling out of bed like I always do on the first day, to help make sure Lexi had everything she needed for the day. I knew she was nervous to start a new school, and with good reason since most of the time we moved a couple weeks before school started. Lexi and I usually spent so much time transferring her IEP and buying last-minute school supplies, that she had no time for meeting new students.

This was the first time in a while where Lexi knew the students in her classes, at least a few of them. She'd spent time all summer working, hanging out at the lake beach, hosting gatherings at Wild Rose House, and it paid off with her having friends before even setting foot on the school campus.

"Backpack, lunchbox, water bottle," I mumbled, roaming around the small house to gather everything. I paused to yawn and stretch, noticing the mess of Manic hair dye we forgot to clean up the previous evening.

I had helped Lexi touch up her pink hair when she decided to keep the color for a little while longer. She figured people recognized her because of her hair, so she didn't want to mess around with it much, being the new girl.

Once she dressed, I plaited Lexi's hair in quick Dutch braids. I watched her in the small bathroom as she chose minimal makeup, opting for just mascara and colored lip gloss. She was gorgeous no matter how much or little she put on her face, but her eyes popped when she tinted her lashes. Eyes that matched mine. She went simple with denim shorts—because it was still hot—and a t-shirt, and of course her signature Chucks. As she was lacing up her shoes, her phone screen lit up with a text from Sophie.

"Tell her hi for me," I said, sliding away to the kitchen to make pancakes. We didn't have enough time for bacon, so I threw some chocolate chips in the pancake mix and told myself it would be fine. If David was there, he would have gotten up early to help and fill the counter with bacon, eggs, pancakes, and fruit. My focus had been coffee and getting Lexi's hair done. Can't do it all, I thought, and shrugged. I looked around and found some bananas, placing them next to the plate of pancakes.

"There, fruit," I said, nodding.

After inhaling chocolate chip pancakes and drinking a cup of coffee, we drove the short distance to Willow High, and I pulled into the drop-off line. Eventually she'd need her own car, but she didn't seem to mind me driving her around until that became a reality. Sophie would drive her to the cafe where they'd share a shift after school was out, and we'd probably be done with our jobs at the same time for us to ride home together. I stopped in front of the school when it was our turn and told her to have a lovely and special and amazing first day.

"Back to the grind," I mumbled, waving to her as she adjusted her backpack and ran off to meet up with Sophie. I fought tears, realizing it was the last first day I'd have with her. I thought back to Kindergarten, having to walk her in the building, her tiny hand grasping mine hard as she fought for bravery. I'd somehow blinked, and she was a senior. I wasn't one to get overly nostalgic normally, but it seemed lately all I could do was sort through memories of the past. Everything came up all at once, all the first day of school memories of dresses and braids and photos in front of the door. There were so many different doors over the years.

I stopped by the cafe on my way to the office. It felt weird without Penny, though I knew I'd see her in a few minutes. More memories swarmed, the good now tangled so much with the bad that it seemed one couldn't exist without the other.

I'd spent a lot of time serving customers and organizing the stockroom. And of course avoiding Penny and any real emotion.

Thinking about my friend, I grabbed an extra coffee and a pastry on my way out. I wanted to surprise her with a show of kindness before hitting her with the heavy schedule for the week. In small town Willow, the first week of school was a busy one.

Chapter 38

"Penny, I brought you coffee," I said as I bustled through the office. "And food. Sugar food. And before you ask, yes, the cafe is doing ok but it'll never be as great without you." I winked at her and she commented about my current caffeine and sugar levels. I shrugged and rolled a chair over to sit next to her.

"Lexi is in her senior year," I said with a sigh. "She's going to leave me soon and I feel like I haven't had enough time with her."

Penny nodded, finishing a bite of her pastry. The silence sat heavily for a moment until she said, "Lexi isn't going to run, Jenna."

I grimaced and sipped my coffee. Penny reached out and touched my hand and I looked up at her, guilt all over my face.

"She's not going to run, and if she leaves she'll come back. You came back," she whispered, squeezing my fingers.

I nodded, not trusting myself to talk.

"Jenna, you came back. And look, we're somehow in charge of this whole damn place," she said gesturing to the building, empty for the moment apart from us. "This job is awesome! Friday, for example, I had an interview with the fire chief about a new truck they were finally getting after raising money for years to save up enough. Then I had to go take photos at the butterfly garden since the new fall blooms were on full display. Today I needed to input a couple stories into the computer for review, and then I had to research and write a story from a couple days ago using the interview notes I'd gotten from a school board meeting. How is this my life?"

I laughed, knowing exactly the excitement she felt after almost 2 decades of working in publishing.

"Some days I have nothing to do," Penny said, and laughed, adding, "Don't tell my boss!"

I missed our easy conversations. I was so glad I asked her to join me on the newspaper staff. She was a fantastic reporter, editor, page designer, photographer; anything I needed her to do she did with a smile and I could tell she actually enjoyed it all.

"OK, I won't tell your boss if you don't tell mine I'm not working either." I suddenly noticed a new photo frame sitting on Penny's desk. "You framed our picture!" I exclaimed, reaching for the photo. It was our new photo with Lauren. We looked so much older and yet just the same as we did when we were kids.

"I still miss Tina too," Penny said to me, before taking in a breath like she hadn't meant to say it out loud.

"It's ok to talk about her," I told her. "It's the year of healing, and part of that is wading through all the muck of memories. I've been in it knee deep since I got back. Things I buried deep are finding their way back to the surface. I don't want you to ever feel like you can't be honest or share things with me, Pen. I'm ok, I promise. No more running."

I reached out and squeezed her fingers like she did mine a few minutes ago.

"You're right," I said, slightly changing the subject back to my kid's senior year. "Lexi won't run. I want her to go to college as close or as far as she wants to, but I know she'll always be on the other end of the phone. Thanks, friend. Now let's probably get back to work before the boss turns us in."

Penny rolled her eyes and pushed me lightly, sending my rolling chair away from her desk. We got back to work, both silent in our tasks, and it felt really good to have her there with me. Eventually the other staffers filtered in and out, dropping off pages or logging into computers. We'd have to hire another couple people soon, which was an amazing problem to have. I wanted to lighten my workload as the school activities amped up. I didn't really believe Lexi would leave me forever, but I still wanted to spend as much time with her as possible while she was still living with me. I wanted to support her, and Sophie too, with anything they needed. We would make so many new memories and adventures.

Chapter 39

1999

Spring Break 1999, before the tragedy changed everything, Dottie did something she never usually did—she drove us teens to an amusement park in Texas. She borrowed a huge van for the occasion and set down I-35 with snacks, pop, and a tank full of gas.

Ty sat up front because he got carsick, and also so my mother could keep an eye on him. He somehow always got in trouble when he was too far out of eyesight. Lauren and Penny sat in the middle, and Tina and I took the back.

We teens chose the music, taking turns between listening to grunge, boy bands, and pop divas. The drive wasn't too bad when everyone sang along and slept when they were bored.

Dottie even played rummy with Ty, Lauren and Penny while she drove, though Ty helped her spread her cards out over the dash and told her what cards were hers to play. It was a different time, and unknown to the group it would be one of the last big fun weeks we'd have all together.

We stopped at a hotel along the way and packed into a cramped room together. There were two beds and a pull-out sofa, so Dottie took one bed to herself—the kids insisted since she was driving and needed good rest—and we used a complex version of rock, paper, scissors to decide who got the second bed. After a bit of arguing over rules and specifics, Lauren and Tina got the bed, Penny and I got the sofa bed, and Ty ended up volunteering to sleep on the floor, anyway. He said he liked the floor. The girls laughed and told him he was ridiculous, and by the grin on Ty's face we figured the reaction he got was why he said he liked the floor.

Overall, the drive was way better than the vacation itself. The amusement park was crowded and Penny got sick from eating too much cotton candy. The weather was pretty good at least—Texas in March—but the clouds made everyone feel cold after a couple splash rides. We spent the night in another hotel and Ty and Tina made up ghost stories to tell before bed. Penny ducked out to get ice from the hallway, emphatically explaining she wasn't afraid. The next day we hung around the hotel, eating Texas shaped waffles for breakfast in the lobby, almost burning popcorn in the room and watching cartoons on cable television. We played at an arcade and ordered pizza for dinner. No one had wanted to go back to the amusement park. We just wanted to be together doing silly things like racing through the hallways and lamenting about lost loves and our favorite shoes that didn't fit anymore.

We were tired on the drive back to Iowa and everyone got a bit cranky. Ty wanted to listen to Pearl Jam the whole way and Lauren had suddenly developed an allergy to all things grunge. They argued about it until Dottie turned on oldies music and told everyone to go to sleep. She stopped at a gas station and bought bottles of ginger ale for everyone. She handed us all Dramamine to keep us from getting sick and to help us fall asleep. That night in the hotel there was more fighting about which teen got which bed, what to watch on tv, and about every other little thing we could think about arguing over.

Dottie took it well, having dealt with the teens' moods before, and she just ordered more pizza and let us work it out. After we all ate, things did seem to get better, and everyone sort of worked together to figure out who would sleep on which surface. Ty took the floor again, claiming he'd always let the girls have the best. His grin calmed everyone else down and we laughed again, sharing funny stories instead of scary ones.

"OH, remember that time last summer with the dog?" Penny exclaimed to the group, looking to me to answer the question.

We had been cleaning up after a summer bonfire on a Saturday morning and kept hearing a noise in the cornfield. We'd see the stalks moving this way and that, and the birds flying and cawing, clearly disturbed by something. All morning we kept seeing small movements and after a while we called it the CFM—Corn Field Monster.

"Look, the CFM is heading that way!" Ty would shout, pointing. What had started as small movements and a curiosity turned into an obsession to figure out what was in there, no matter how dangerous.

We slowly walked toward the CFM, Penny staying behind the rest of us, shaking and whining that they should go get a grownup.

"Back off Penny, but do NOT go get Dottie," Tina said harshly. "This is our adventure, and we're going to capture the monster." She giggled and held a blanket in front of her, ready to drop it on whatever was making the noise.

A few steps later the movement stopped. No stalks shuffling. No birds cawing and flying away. Everything got quiet.

"Shhhh, it's over here," Ty said, leading the group. I nodded to Tina, and we moved ahead of Lauren with the blanket. Smiling at each other, we stopped to listen. "We'll get the CFM if it's the last thing we do," Ty said, earning more giggles from the girls. He peeked in the stalks where the noise had stopped and paused for effect.

"What is it?" Lauren whispered. Penny whimpered.

"Shhhh, let me get closer," Ty whispered back. He took a couple more steps into the stalks, holding a hand behind him.

Waiting a few more seconds, I made eye contact, and he winked and smiled, giving me the only hint I'd need to play along. Loudly to the rest of the group he yelled, "Oh my GOD, get out of here! GO, GO!" The girls screamed and ran, Penny crying and the rest scared until they saw Ty's face.

"I got you SO good," he laughed, causing Tina to smack his arm and call him a name. "For real though, there's something there and you'll never believe what."

I reached in and coaxed out a scared puppy, dirty and obviously lost. The girls awwwed, even Penny, who had recovered quickly from the scare.

We took turns holding the puppy in the blanket and gave him a bowl of water and some turkey slices from our lunch sandwiches. We played with CFM for an hour or more until Dottie came out to check on us and saw our new friend.

"We can't keep him, kids," she said right away, patting the dog on the head. "He might belong to someone. I'll take him in to the vet to see about a chip or a missing dog bulletin."

With that, she'd crushed our dreams of having a dog. But the memory of the CFM lived on, and we forever considered the story of the hotel room on Spring Break 1999 to be epic, the stuff of legends.

Chapter 40

The weekend after school started was a celebration at Wild Rose House. I taught Lexi that summer that any time there could be a celebration, there was one. We weren't sure if it was a small town Iowa thing, a Willow thing, or just a Wild Rose House thing, but we loved it all the same.

We spent Saturday afternoon getting things ready for another bonfire that evening. This time we had invited everyone. Ty was driving in from Iowa City, Dottie and Charles had friends from church coming, and I had made sure Lauren and Penny knew they could bring any friends they had outside of our group. Sophie was bringing a date and Lexi made Matty promise he'd be there too. She told him he could bring friends, but no alcohol. I had to draw the line somewhere. I promised lots of food and non-alcoholic drinks though.

Sophie and Lauren showed up first, bringing bags of marshmallows and boxes of Graham crackers.

"I hope you have chocolate bars, because I completely forgot them," Lauren told me, rolling her eyes. "I'm getting old. Someone stop this." She winked at Lexi, who smiled and hugged her cousin.

I called out from my mountain of things—tables, tablecloths, plastic forks and spoons, plates, bowls, cups, and who knows what else—that it was ok she forgot chocolate bars because Lexi would go get them.

"Here, take these keys," I told her, tossing a set of keys Lexi hadn't seen before. She caught them and raised an eyebrow, confused only for a second before squealing in excitement, hoping it meant what she thought it did.

"Calm down, little one," I told her in a singsong voice. "It's nothing special. I got a good deal on a used car and I figured you could test it out today, see how it drives. Just to the store and back ok? With an adult!" I grabbed the cases of pop and began filling them in coolers already filled with ice. "Lauren?" I called out to my cousin.

"I'm on it," she said to me, grabbing her purse. "I call shotgun!" She winked at me and turned to Lexi. "We're not letting you take out a car you've never driven before without a grownup, duh. Now go, I want to get back before everyone gets here. This party's going to be so fun tonight."

They left, and I grinned, unable to stop the feeling. I'd just let my daughter take a car out with family members, something I'd never thought I'd see just a few short months ago.

I'd just about finished loading the pop into the cooler when my phone chimed, letting me know someone was video calling.

"David! Oh, you'll never believe what just happened!" He laughed and told me Lexi had just text him a photo of a beat up Jeep.

"You got the deal!" he said, smiling. We'd talked at length about what type of vehicle to get and whether it was a good idea to let her drive at all.

"It's 4 wheel drive for when it snows. You know that girl won't know what to do when those first flakes hit the ground."

David nodded. "I'm not sure I'd know what to do either," he laughed. "This Texas boy can't hang in the snow. What are ya'll up to this afternoon? I think it's afternoon, right?" He'd obviously been sleeping when Lexi text him.

"What's it like in the future?" I asked, winking. "Here in the past, we're doing a bonfire tonight. The girls made it through their first week of school unscathed and we think that's worth celebrating. I think Dottie's invited the whole town though. I don't know that we even have enough space for everyone!"

I'd told him about our bonfires, and he knew they could get rowdy.

"Is Ty coming?" he asked. I nodded.

"He's on his way. He should be here in..." I glanced at her watch. "About 30 minutes. He says he's bringing someone." I grinned, unable to hide my happiness. "We've literally never seen him with anyone, ever. He apparently dates a lot and said he was a superstar back in high school, but we honestly have never seen him with another human. He keeps that information on strict lockdown. I'm so happy he's finally sharing his life with us."

David nodded again. "I think you had something to do with that," he reminded me. "You brought everyone back together and shared your own life with them. It makes it easier, I think. Don't you?"

We chatted a bit more and suddenly everyone started showing up. I held the phone up so David could see Lexi running over with her set of keys and the chocolate bars they'd gone to get. Lauren and Sophie waved to the camera and said they couldn't wait to meet him in person. Everyone yelled their hellos until a series of honks interrupted them.

"Ty's here!" I yelled, knowing the honks the way I knew his knocks. Ty just had a way about him like that. "Lexi, he said he's bringing someone." We watched for Ty to walk from the driveway around the house. He peeked out and, upon seeing us, ran over and grabbed us all in a group hug. I almost dropped my phone and instantly felt sorry for the headache I probably gave David with all the spinning. I smirked at the screen and David's body shook in laughter. We all looked up at a man in his mid 40s walking slowly, almost shyly, toward us. Ty grabbed his hand and introduced him as his boyfriend, Nathaniel.

With tears in my eyes, I handed the phone to my daughter and rushed in to give this new person a giant hug of welcome.

"It's so nice to meet you, Nathaniel. I'm sorry this level of familiarity is what you're jumping into today, but we're just so happy to have you here." I reached out and squeezed Ty's hand, nodding and winking in approval of the handsome stranger.

"He's cute," I whispered. "Well done, my friend." I giggled and grabbed my phone back from Lexi.

"David, we love you! We'll talk to you again soon! I'll call you tomorrow and debrief!" I told him goodbye and put my phone back in my pocket.

Penny walked up, holding a bottle of wine. She had a nervous look on her face, eyes going back and forth between everyone. She noticed Ty holding hands with a new gentleman and let out an anxious breath, smiling.

"Um," she started, laughing nervously. "I guess I missed Ty's introduction. I'm Penny. The not-cousin one." The two shook hands and Ty rolled his eyes ceremoniously. His dramatics dripped as he repeated Penny's words.

"The not-cousin one," he said. "Oh my God, Penny, get over yourself and realize you're a freaking part of this dumb group, whether you like it or not!"

He grabbed Penny in a bear hug until she giggled and gave in, admitting she's a Wild Rose Girl. Lauren and I laughed and cheered, everyone else not sure what was happening. I forgot how crazy we got when we were together.

"Oh, Jenna, I have a surprise for you!" Penny said, sobering a bit. She reached into her bag and pulled out an envelope, handing it to her friend with a smirk. "I really hope that banishment is not on the table, because this might do me in."

I took the envelope slowly, a cringe on my face.

"Banishment worthy? What'd you do now?"

I read the letter carefully, multiple times, before passing it around the family circle. I was quiet while everyone read it and once everyone had, they all looked to me, waiting.

"Say something!" Penny whispered. "Please."

I opened my mouth and closed it again, gathering my thoughts.

"Let me get this right," I started slowly. "You wrote the city a letter asking them to apologize for their wrongdoing 20 something years ago about an event they might not even remember, and they wrote you back with an actual apology and a motion to add new benches around the square in Tina's memory?"

Penny nodded slowly, unsure of my mood. "Um, yes, I did do that, and yes, they did do that."

I took a deep breath and held it in for a moment, letting my eyes close. When I opened them they were wet with tears. I looked to Ty, who was tearing up as well. He nodded to me, unable to speak.

"Penny, you did well, friend," I whispered, my voice cracking. "Thank you. I don't know what we did to deserve a family like this one, but I'm so very thankful for it."

We did one more group hug, and I wiped my tears, telling them to stop the mushy stuff.

"We can always sue the city instead, you know," Lauren said, only half kidding. "I mean, I know a guy, is all I'm saying. Benches are nice, but I bet we could get a lot more if you want to push a little."

I waved a hand in front of my face and shook my head.

"Not now! We have a bonfire to finish! Everyone else will be here in just a bit! Go, get to work!" I pushed them all to their assignments and hugged myself for a moment, taking it all in. I read the letter from the city again and placed it in my pocket.

"Let's bonfire!"

Chapter 41

The bonfire was in full swing, with adults and teens all over the yard. Dottie had already heard from the neighbors about the noise, but I heard her tell them to lighten up and come over.

"Stop being old and let's do one last party!" she said on the phone. I about lost it listening to her, and ended up fully unable to hide my laughter. She saw me laughing and winked, yelling, "YOLO!" She'd been hanging around Lexi too much.

I looked over at Lexi and her friends. It was tough to hear everyone, but they seemed to do ok. Lots of smiles and food being thrown around between them.

"Matty plays the guitar!" one teenager yelled to Lexi. "Ask him to play. He's always got that shit in the back of his truck. He never goes anywhere without it!" Lexi looked at her boyfriend with amazement.

"You did NOT tell me this fact!" she yelled to him across the table of food. "Go, right now, get this supposed guitar. I won't be deprived of this for any longer." She dramatically pointed to where everyone parked the vehicles, trying not to crack a smile. Matt blushed and shrugged, jogging off to get the guitar. "So much I still don't know about him," she said to Sophie, laughing.

We were getting everyone settled in the backyard. The nights were still long, so it wouldn't get dark for a while, but we started the fire and everyone settled in on a log, bench, or blanket. The adults sat on folding chairs and Charles had even had two of the teenage boys from the football team drag his recliner outside. He'd asked in jest but the boys took it as a challenge and made it happen. Charles smirked and said he felt like the king of the bonfire as he leaned back and got comfortable. I couldn't help but smile at my dad looking about as relaxed and talkative as I'd ever seen him.

Matt came back with his instrument and gave Lexi a kiss on the cheek before sitting down on a log beside her. He started playing, and it turned out he was fantastic. Emmy and Sophie started singing along with the song, and soon enough most of the teens joined in, laughing, yelling the words, pointing at each other and really hamming it up. When he got to a slow romantic song, Lexi watched him shyly as he played and sang himself. He was bold and confident with the guitar in his hands and Lexi looked like she really liked that side of him. When he finished, he set his guitar down beside him and cleared his throat, his self confidence waning. He smirked at Lexi and she told him he needed to play for her every single day for the rest of time. Matty blushed at the sentiment and Lexi leaned in to kiss him softly.

It was a sweet moment that I almost missed, if not for Penny elbowing me and nodding her head toward them. I smiled at my daughter, truly happy for her. It was a beautiful thing watching love grow. I trusted them both to treat each other well, but I knew I'd be there for her if and when she needed me. Looking around, I realized they'd all be there for her. Lexi had so many loved ones on her side waiting to build her up, catch her if she fell, and support her every step of her life, from then on.

Penny smiled knowingly at me and whispered, "I'm sorry David couldn't be here. I know you miss him so much." I nodded, thanking her.

"I'm happy you're here," I told her, leaning my head toward hers. "I know we haven't hoped too much for good things for a while, but trust me when I say it's ok to hope. It's ok to be happy. In all my misery, I met David, and created that beautiful human right there. The feelings can exist together and in spite of each other. Be happy, Pen." I grabbed her hand and squeezed, and Penny returned the squeeze, tears in her eyes.

"I am happy," she said, thinking about it for a moment. "I'm not sure when it happened, but day by day I just started choosing life for myself. You know I always followed you around when we were kids. I wanted your decisions to be my decisions. I wanted your hobbies and favorite things to be mine too. When you left... I didn't know who I even was on my own. Jenna, I was so alone. We all lost Tina that summer, but we didn't realize we'd lost you too. You just... left us."

I nodded, knowing the pain she'd caused by running. "I'm so sorry Pen. You know why I left, but I hope you also know why I came back. Look at all this, look at what we have. How can anyone stay away from this? Even Ty made the drive. He's having a blast! I wonder when is the last time he let himself feel happy?" We looked over at Ty and Nathaniel, dancing like the teenagers around them, singing along with the music on the boombox someone turned on. He looked so much like the Ty we remembered—ornery, happy, the life of the party. Infectious happiness.

"Pen, I can't bring back all these years of silence between us... but I really hope we can spend our old lady years together. Look at Dottie and her friends. We're looking at our future. Yikes," I laughed, pointing at Dottie sitting beside Charles, yelling to her old ladies about the youth music choices.

Lauren approached then, slightly breathless. "I don't want to alarm anyone, but I hear something in the corn. I think it's a CFM." Penny and I looked at each other and laughed loudly.

"NO, not a CFM!" Penny exclaimed, louder than she meant to. Lexi overheard and raised an eyebrow in question.

"Uh, Penny, what exactly is a CFM? Did I hear that right?" Lexi asked. She and Sophie got up to see why the ladies gathered and what we were on about. "In the corn? Sophie, I told you something would come out of there and kill us someday."

Ty had the boys lower the music and sauntered over to the group. "Move over ladies, your knight in shining armor has arrived."

"Ty is our CFM catcher," I explained. Lexi asked what that word meant, and I stifled a laugh. "It's the Corn Field Monster, and shhhhh look, Ty's headed over. Let's follow."

The teens looked at each other, curious and a bit scared but refusing to admit it. Ty went in first, followed by Lauren and me with a blanket in front of us. Lexi and Sophie were next. Penny, always the scared one even when she knows what's happening, stayed at the rear with Nathaniel, who was unsure whether this was real or some kind of joke.

"OK, Ty, like last time, yeah? You go in and I'm right behind you." I followed Ty into the stalks, the teens shining their cell phone flashlights to light their way. "Lauren, can you go let Dottie know we're looking for the CFM so she doesn't get scared when we find it?" I asked, winking. Lauren nodded and gave a salute, leaving them to their task.

"Mom, be careful! Geez, I heard something! Over there!" Lexi pointed out an area to the right where the stalks moved, rustling on their own. "Matty, you better not let me die, or I swear I'll come back and haunt you..." Matt put his arms around her and promised he'd have her back. With a kiss on her cheek he held her to him and smiled. "You big dumb oaf," she told him, smiling back at him. "Thank you."

The source of the noise shuffled the stalks again, and Ty and Jenna went toward it. Ty moved the corn stalks slowly and he and I looked at each other before I nodded and screamed, "Monster!"

My yell sent the teens running back toward the house, screaming too. Everyone rushed back but turned to see what was going to come at them. They saw Ty and me laughing hysterically and everyone turned to each other, smirking.

"You should see your faces!" I said, tears running down my face. "I'm sorry, Lex, but we got you so gooooood!" I fell to the ground laughing and Lexi dropped next to me, laughing too.

"What the HELL, Mom!" she yelled at me, going back and forth between being mad and laughing at me acting like a teenager.

Ty walked out with the blanket, and put a finger to his mouth, shhhhhing.

"There's actually something in there?" Lexi asked, whispering loudly. "What is it?"

Ty pulled back the blanket to show a little pup. Dottie shuffled through the crowd, seeing Ty and me at the center of the prank. Upon seeing the dog, she rolled her eyes and threw her hands up.

"Oh, for Pete's sake, not again," she said, but then smiled. "I'll call the vet."

Lexi mouthed, "Again?" as I stepped in front of my mother.

"You'll do no such thing, Mom," I told her, crossing my arms. "Not this time."

Lexi threw her hands over her mouth, laughing at her mother standing up to her grandmother. No one told Dottie no. She elbowed Sophie to make sure she was watching.

"Jenna, you can't keep a dog! What do you know about taking care of... oh, goodness what am I doing. Girl, you're 40 years old. Do what you want. But you're cleaning up every mess that dog makes!" Dottie backed down, smiling at her daughter.

I jumped up and down and took the bundled blanket from Ty. I snuggled the blanket close to me and started whispering to the puppy.

Lexi inched closer to us, unsure of what was happening.

"Lexi, we've encountered a CFM before, and your gramma made us give him to the vet, who found him a family that was not us. This time, we keep him." I pulled the little dog out of the blanket. "Oh, sorry, we keep her. Assuming she isn't tagged. I guess we do still need the vet. But she's ours!"

The crowd went back to the bonfire, still laughing at the prank Ty pulled. The teenage boys clapped him on the back and called him the man. Nathaniel snuggled closer to him, proud of his date. "My man," he said, chuckling.

I looked around the fire at all my favorite people gathered. Lexi sat with Matty, his arm around her. Sophie was next to her with Emmy and some boys I was sure would be traded out for new ones next week. Lauren sat with Dottie and Charles, talking about real estate prices and the latest trends in 60+ community living. Penny sat on the ground near me, leaning against a hay bale and fighting sleep. Ty and Nathaniel were arm in arm on a log bench. I looked down to the little girl pup in my lap. My little CFM.

This was the stuff of legends. My family surrounding me. My trauma healing. My business thriving. My daughter happy.

I thought back to that drive from San Antonio, and the fear I'd felt in my gut. I'd had no way of knowing whether my experiment would work, or if we'd end up running away again.

Now, looking around the backyard, at Wild Rose House, I felt a calm I just couldn't feel anywhere else. I took a deep breath in and shed a tear or two, whispering thoughts of love and a thank you to Tina for showing me the way back home.

Chapter 42

"Lexi, oh my God, we have to get to the airport. We're going to miss the whole thing!" I ran through the house grabbing all the things I needed, which were scattered everywhere. "This is the dumbest deployment pickup ever. Why did we think we could pick him up in San Antonio when we're not even in the right state!"

Lexi calmly walked through the house behind me, gathering her own things, knowing my freakout was just part of the process. We'd fly from Des Moines to San Antonio, meet David at the airport, and drive the rental car to the base so he could check in and drop his things off. We'd stay overnight, and fly back to Des Moines the next day together, in plenty of time for Lexi's graduation weekend. Lexi was missing two days of school for this, but she was pretty much already done with everything minus the exams she'd take at the end of the week.

"This is Monday, right? Lexi, why aren't you freaking out?" I stopped and looked at her when I realized she tricked me. Lexi, newly 18 and smirking fabulously, just shrugged.

"You did it again, didn't you? OK, what time are we ACTUALLY supposed to be at the airport?" I walked away groaning loudly, mumbling about my daughter constantly gaslighting me. I checked my flight time, checked my watch, and did the math to figure out when we needed to be at the airport. Of course we had plenty of time. Lexi had told me we needed to leave by 8am but we didn't really need to leave until 9. I was thankful but also annoyed.

Lexi giggled and helped me finish packing and get our things ready. She had her sign ready, we'd printed out the tickets ahead of time, and we were only packing carry-on bags. I suppose we could have done that trip in our sleep if it hadn't been for my intense nerves.

I hadn't seen David in almost a year.

We put our things in the Jeep and Lexi drove to the airport, parking in the short-term lot since we'd only be gone a day. We'd thought about asking Lauren or Sophie to drive us but we wanted to have our own vehicle ready when they got home.

"Home," I thought, smiling. I wasn't sure exactly when I'd started calling Iowa home, but the thought warmed me. It had been a long year, and I missed David terribly, but it had also been one of the best years of my life. I looked at Lexi and assumed she felt the same. Happiness and excitement radiated from her.

The airport in Des Moines was on the smaller side, so we got through security smoothly and quickly and made it to the gate in time to grab a coffee and snacks. Lexi's ears always hurt on landing and the muted sound echoed for at least half an hour, but she grabbed gum and some Sour Patch Kids, her favorite travel candy, and told me she'd be fine.

The time between our flight landing and David's landing was minimal, and we needed to rush a bit to make it to his gate before he deplaned. He wasn't coming home with a large group, but there were a few of them on the flight. I waved to the other families and pointed to their signs, giving them a thumbs up. When the soldiers walked through the gate, there was cheering and hugging and bystanders clapped and welcomed everyone home, thanking them for their service.

David opened his arms wide for his two favorite girls, giving us both a giant hug before kissing Lexi on the head and taking a bit more time with me. I blushed and told him I was so glad to see him. The homecoming was our favorite part, but it was always tiring. David drew an electric razor out of his pocket and winked at Lexi. She rolled her eyes, telling him she was too old for this tradition, but grabbed the razor anyway. He bent down and held his hands below his chin. She shaved his deployment mustache off like she did every time. After a year this time, it was the thickest it'd ever been, and I giggled as I watched my adult size daughter struggle to get it all cleaned off his face. David just smiled and pretended it wasn't uncomfortable until she was done. He threw away the hair clippings, and I held up a hand mirror I'd pulled from my bag so he could finish the shave. He high-fived Lexi and told her he was officially home.

I picked up our rental car and David drove us all to the base. The gate guards welcomed him back and saluted him through the gate, and then we dropped all his stuff off in his office. He'd sort it all out later, and would have to get back to work eventually, but he had some time off to re-acclimate with his family and it was absolute pure luck that his leave fell over Lexi's graduation.

We got two hotel rooms for obvious reasons and Lexi spent the night texting Matty and Sophie in a mess of hotel snacks on the large bed, already missing them. Her late night showed in the morning, but the Texas shaped waffles in the hotel lobby made it all worth it.

David text Lexi to meet in the breakfast area, where they made waffles.

"Why do these always just taste better?" he asked, smiling at his daughter, who nodded in agreement. "It's nice to see you in the morning again, kiddo." Lexi grunted, her mouth full of waffle. I shuffled in beside them, going straight for coffee. I looked at them both, pointing to the coffeemaker in question. David shook his head but Lexi nodded, indicating she would love to have a cup. There was no question she was a mini version of me.

"So, we don't have long in the city I guess," David said. Lexi was still shoving waffles and bacon into her mouth and grunted again. "It's too bad we need to get you back to school and graduation! It might have been nice to hang around here for a bit." He gestured outside, toward the Riverwalk and the city. "It's so good to be home."

Lexi swallowed her food and rolled her eyes. "I mean, this isn't really home anymore, at least not for us."

David nodded, his forehead scrunching. The reality of the homecoming was that David didn't have a home. They'd packed up the San Antonio house when the lease was up, and by the time David got back, his family had settled almost 1000 miles away in a home he'd never seen. He wouldn't know where the silverware drawer was, or where we kept the extra toothpaste. He would fit in around them, as it has to happen.

"This one seems hard for me, kiddo," he told her. "I'm coming back and ya'll are living in a different state, graduating from a school I've never seen, living in a house I've never lived in. And then you're off to college in a few short months. I think I might need some grace with this one, OK?" Lexi reached out and patted his arm, nodding in agreement.

I approached slowly, having heard the conversation on my way to the table. I placed Lexi's coffee down and kissed David at his temple. I always hated this part of homecoming too. It was a tough transition sharing our home again and allowing someone else to fill in the spaces I'd already claimed in his absence. No doubt we'd have a few arguments and need to respect each other's processes coming back together. Military life wasn't an easy one, but we'd been at it for so long, I was sure we'd continue to do it well, even through this bigger challenge.

"We know the ropes, and we'll work through it together like we always do," I reminded them, grinning. "We know it's going to be hard, but I'm just so happy to have us all together while we can be." I couldn't help the grin that spread across my face, with my two favorite people on either side of me.

Now I just needed to make sure David felt welcome in our new life, whatever that would look like with his job being in Texas and mine being in Iowa.

I grimaced a moment but fixed my face, needing to be strong for the two of them. I fell right back into my military wife routine, and though something felt off about it this time, I smiled through it and focused on my giant waffle.

Things would work out. Somehow.

Chapter 43

Lexi drove us back to Wild Rose House, feeling very adult and in charge for once. I honestly couldn't believe she was 18 and about to graduate high school. Pulling up to the driveway of the big house, she parked and turned to David in the passenger seat.

"Time to put on your big boy pants and remember that this has been our home for a year, ok? It's going to feel small, we're going to crowd each other, and we'll argue over the space in the fridge and where you put your shoes. There's one bathroom. We know all that. But you got this."

I smirked and David raised an eyebrow at me, trying not to laugh from the back seat.

Lexi opened the door and ran to greet Dottie, who held a leash attached to a very clean little pup with a spot over her eye and a tongue hanging out of her mouth. The pup jumped up at the sight of her favorite teen and Lexi opened her arms wide to catch her.

"And we have a dog. He came from a cornfield," she said, carrying little Monster. She reached up to kiss her grama on the cheek and told her hello. David's eyebrow raised again, but he stayed quiet, smirking a little at how his daughter's confidence had grown the past year. It was one thing seeing it her letters and over a phone call, but quite another seeing it in person.

We continued toward Wild Rose House, Lexi pointing out all her favorite parts of the property along the way.

"Here's where we had our bonfires and over there is where CFM showed up. I almost died in the snow over there." She pointed as she walked, rubbing the Monster's back as she went. "Did you know that sledding can be dangerous?" she asked, smirking. "I thought I broke my arm at the bottom of that hill!"

I wrapped my arm around David's and leaned into him. He had missed a lot, that's for sure. He'd gotten small stories in emails and over phone calls, but looking around, he still felt like a stranger, a visitor in a life that didn't belong to him.

"Show me where we're staying," he pushed, eager to catch a nap. The jet lag got to him and he yawned, his body betraying him.

I slid my fingers through David's, smiling at their exchange. I let Lexi run point on the tour, hoping she wasn't overwhelming her father too much. I reached an arm toward the small house and motioned Lexi to continue.

"OK, so this..." Lexi paused and motioned with her free hand like a game show host. "This is Wild Rose House. It's so cute, right? Grama helped me plant these flowers out here, and Grampa had to fix a window after Matty busted it with a baseball." She noticed her dad's grimace and smirked. "It was an accident, and he offered to pay for the replacement, I promise!"

David had actually been grimacing about the boyfriend, not the window, but he chuckled and nodded.

"So if we go inside..." She paused again for effect, opening the door and waiting for us to walk inside. "You can see where we've lived for the last 12 months. Welcome home, Dad!" The dog licked her face, excited at Lexi's excitement. She waited for David to close the door and let the little pup off the leash. The Monster zoomed around the couch a couple times before sliding on the kitchen floor toward her water bowl.

David looked around at the small space, with the couch looming in the middle of the room. The small kitchen was on his right, open to the living area. He could see the small hallway where the bedrooms and bathroom likely were. The home looked like a mix of what he assumed was Dottie's style and that of his wife and daughter. Nothing looked like him in the space, but he was happy to see they'd been safe and comfortable while he was away.

He hugged Lexi and me one more time and told us he loved us but needed a nap before he dropped. I showed him to the bedroom and Lexi tended to the pup, texting Matty and Sophie to let them know she'd made it back.

The rest of the week was pretty uneventful; I went to work each morning and Lexi went to school and took her final exams. David stayed back at the house answering emails and trying to regulate his sleep cycle to match central time zone.

Lexi studied hard and finished her finals feeling like she'd nailed them, and we'd had a small family party Friday night so David could meet the whole crew. Ty drove to town with Nathaniel for Lexi and Sophie's graduation, Penny was happy as ever on her own, and Lauren was still happily Dink-free. Sophie, Emmy, Matty and Dottie and Charles rounded out the group, and David happily admitted he'd liked them all. He could immediately see why we had bonded with this place, with these people. We were a tight group but very welcoming. He had a special look and nod for the other "outsider" Nathaniel, as they both understood the honor it was to be included.

Saturday morning was a rush. I ran around looking for my watch, and my phone, and my shoes, as if they weren't all in the same place I always left them. Lexi was a sea of calm, getting ready slowly and methodically. David made breakfast for everyone, having felt much better after a couple days of extra naps and acclimating. He whistled as he cooked, inviting Lexi to help him in the kitchen. I smiled constantly; it'd been so long since I'd woken up to David whistling over a pan of sizzling bacon.

"Good morning, Dad," Lexi said, stealing a piece of bacon from the pile cooling on a plate beside the stove. "Mom's in freakout mode again." David nodded, chuckling, watching me zoom in and out of the kitchen and through the living room.

"She'll calm down with some food," he told his daughter. "Jenna, come sit before you wear holes into the floors! Food is ready!" His voice carried through the house and I came marching in seconds, hungry and happy to stop pacing.

We finished breakfast and once everyone dressed we gathered in front of the door, holding hands and taking some deep breaths together—our family huddle.

I had curled my hair, which I'd let grow long, gray just barely starting to highlight my shiny brown locks at my temples. I felt pretty in minimal makeup and a flowy sundress. I held a wrap and a small purse. Lexi and I looked down at our huddled feet, noticing each other's favorite shoes. Heels would never cut it for us no matter our ages, and we winked at each other's constant aversion to any uncomfortable footwear. Lexi chose a flowy dress similar to mine, which she'd cover with her graduation gown. She had put half her hair up in a fancy clip, curling the rest that flowed down long over her shoulders—still pastel pink—so she could wear her graduation cap overtop. Her makeup was fun, with hints of brightness in her purple and silver eyeshadow and liner. She wore a little blush and some sheer pink lipstick, making her green eyes stand out.

"Ladies, we've worked hard for this. Are we good? Ready?" David looked back and forth from Lexi to me. We both nodded and smiled, squeezing each other's hands. "Good. Now we get this girl graduated!"

Lexi squealed at the thought, and her whole face lit up in a grin. She shot Sophie, Emmy, and Matt quick texts and practically ran to the car, the very SUV she and I had driven to Iowa almost exactly a year ago.

When we got to the school, I had an intense moment of déjà vu. We parked, walked in, and Lexi ran to Matty and her friends, jumping up and down in excitement. That part is definitely different, I thought with a smirk.

"Are we going to have another runner?" Dottie asked, stepping up to us watching our daughter walking to the senior hold room. Charles stood behind her, grasping David's hand in a shake and giving a nod of a hello.

"Mom, I didn't realize you were capable of humor!" I teased, play hitting my mom on the shoulder. "Thank you for being here. It means everything to that girl—and to me." I squeezed my mom's hand and looked down in embarrassment. "I know the last time we set foot here it didn't go so well. But no, I don't think we have a runner. She's better than me in every single way." I winked.

Dottie clicked her tongue and waved her hand, saying, "Oh, I wouldn't say she's better than you in everything. Well, maybe at getting flowers to live." She laughed. "I guess I'm what the kids call 'on fire' today with my jokes, yeah?" She looked to David and chuckled.

"Hello, David," she said to him. "I hope you've settled a bit. Congratulations on your homecoming and having gotten your daughter this far. Now let's hope she really doesn't pull her mother's card today. I really don't want to deal with another Wild Rose Girl running off in front of everyone." She touched her head, as if the very thought was giving her a headache. She shook her head and hit back at me lightly. "Jenna embarrassed us all with her little stunt. I'm amazed we got her inside this building at all."

I bit my lip and looked around. "Trust me, I'm still considering running," I said, and then took a deep breath. "Let's go find our seats."

We found our assigned seats near the rest of the family and waited patiently for our graduate.

As the Seniors all walked in and found their chairs, the crowd gave a quick cheer of support. I waved at Lexi and Sophie, giving them both a thumbs up and then an "I Love You" sign. The girls both blew kisses back and turned to listen to the principal introduce the Class of 2024.

After the principal's speech, he introduced the class president and the Valedictorian, who both gave short but wonderful speeches of their own. Next the principal introduced a special guest speaker.

"We normally don't have another speaker, but we had to bend the rules with this one. This year we had a student join us in a time of absolute chaos. She began her senior year in a new state with her father deployed. She jumped right in and immediately joined clubs, studied hard, and thrived here with us. Now her dad has come home! Please welcome him and also give a big round of applause for our Lexi Abbott!"

Lexi stood up, looking nervous. She walked toward the stage as the crowd clapped, everyone loving a good military homecoming story. Like her mother over two decades ago, she paused at the threshold, as if she considered running. I drew in a sharp breath, holding it until I saw my daughter's foot hit the stair, heading up to the stage. I let it out slowly, reaching for David's hand.

Facing the small crowd, Lexi smiled and adjusted the microphone, clearing her throat in preparation, giving her a few seconds to clear her head as well.

One deep breath in and out, and Lexi was ready.

"Hello everyone, thank you for letting me take a few minutes of your time before your loved ones walk the stage for the last time. I can't believe we all made it this far but here we are!" She paused a moment for applause before continuing.

"You probably don't know me. I'm Lexi Abbott, and this is my first, last, and only year here at Willow High. My mom Jenna Rose Abbott almost stood here 20 some years ago as Valedictorian of her class, but she went on a little run instead. I'm here all these years later in honor of her. Everyone loves to tell me how proud they are of my father for his almost two decades of military service, and I'm so so proud of him too. But I wanted to take a few minutes today to talk about my mom's resilience and to tell you about a girl who never made it to graduation at all."

She looked at our family, at her friends, and began the story of twins, one of whom died too young. She talked about her mother's trauma; choosing to run from the pain. I lowered my head, embarrassed again at the memories.

"In that running, in that pain, my mother met a dashing young man who would take her around the world with military service. They would have a baby and give her everything. When times got the darkest, when that military service would take my dad away for a year during arguably the toughest year to raise a teenager, my mother realized the one thing she hadn't given me: family."

She gestured to the members of the front rows, all smiling at her.

"I have been all over. I have had so many opportunities to grow and learn and thrive. And yet it took a rowdy bunch of traumatized adults and a cornfield monster for me to truly shine. Who knew I would find a home among the boredom of Willow?" She paused with a small laugh. "Who knew I would truly FIND myself among the people in a small town in a flyover state?"

She gestured to the whole audience.

"Please remember, class of 2024, no matter how far you go, no matter how big you get or what great things you accomplish, your home is here. We'll always have these people, this place, to come back and hug us when we need some love. If we mess up, if we run away, if we get our hearts broken or fail at a goal we set, we always have Willow. We always have family—both blood and found."

With that she nodded to the principal and sighed, smiling shyly at her classmates.

Sophie was the first to stand, clapping. Matty whistled loudly and the whole room of people joined in, cheering.

I smiled through the tears streaming down my face. Everyone sat back down, and the graduation continued, each Senior walking across the stage upon hearing their name, with a renewed sense of accomplishment on their faces.

I hadn't been able to feel this at my own graduation, but sitting there in the stuffy warm auditorium watching my daughter begin her adult life, none of it mattered.

Lexi was right. She'd always have Willow. She'd always have Home.

-The End-

Epilogue

2025

"Matty, one more box! Do you think you can grab it, love?" Lexi called out, her arms full. Her boyfriend called out that he'd get it, and hoisted the box into his arm, keeping one hand free to open the door. "Thank you!" Lexi told him, sliding through the doorway with her bags threatening to topple. She stopped to kiss Matt and the top of her pile slid. He caught it easily and made a joke about always being there to put out her fires.

"Hey, I'm the calm one," Lexi reminded him. "I'm just clumsy."

They left the Freshman dorm, piling everything into her Jeep and his truck. He'd lived on the 5th floor, and she and Sophie shared a suite with Emmy on the 4th. Matt had been jealous all year of the girls' private bathroom, when everyone else with single and double rooms had to share the hall bathroom.

Lexi was one of the last to leave the dorm, having had late finals. Matt had waited around to help her load everything, promising to follow her back to Willow.

"Hey Matty, we made it through our first year at Iowa State, and you aren't tired of me yet! We should celebrate tonight. Pizza and ice cream?" She waited at her vehicle, driver door open, for him to answer.

He ran to her and pulled her up into a bear hug, kissing her on the way down. "I could never get sick of you, ever," he told her. "Yes, to pizza and ice cream. Yes to you." He jogged back to his truck, turning to her so she could see him say, "I'll meet you back home."

Home. Yes, back to Willow. A lot had happened this past year, that's for sure. Lexi text her mom to tell her she would be home in about an hour, and she drove back, Matty keeping his promise to follow her the whole way.

They pulled into the driveway and Lexi practically tore the door open to get out and run to David and me, who were waiting at the porch of the big house. She enveloped us in a big hug, struggling to get words out to say hello.

"How's the big house treating you?" she asked. We'd finally moved everything in a few weeks ago and Lexi hadn't actually seen it since everything went from belonging to the Roses to belonging to the Abbotts. "I want to know everything. Take me on the whole tour. Oh, Matty's here, too. He's coming with," she said in her take-charge way, putting her arm through Matt's and hugging his side. David and Matt shook hands and nodded to each other, smiling at Lexi's announcement.

"Can't argue with the boss," Matt said, laughing and pulling Lexi in closer. "Let's go."

I pointed out all the things I'd changed, making the house less stuffy and more homey. "No offense to your grandmother," I said with a smirk.

"Oh, I think Dottie and Charles are just fine with it," David chimed in. "They're quite the hit at their new seniors-only neighborhood Lauren set them up with. We'll go visit them later and you can see what I mean."

Lexi laughed with him and said, "Dottie is in charge everywhere she goes. Where do you think I learned it from?" With a wink, she threw her hands out and told us we'd done an outstanding job.

"Dad, are you here full-time yet?" she asked him. He'd put in for retirement, as it'd officially been 20 years of service. "You have, what, 3 weeks left?" David nodded and told her he needed to go back in a few days to finish everything, but then he'd be able to stop the back and forth flights from San Antonio to Des Moines.

There had been a lot of conversations between David and me about where to land once retirement is a certain thing. I was adamant about staying in Iowa, a choice David was apprehensive about at first. Before I'd reconnected with my family, we'd always talked about staying in Texas, where David had grown up. His parents were gone, and he'd been an only child, but the area was familiar to him and after two decades of moving around, the military had finally sent them back to his home. He didn't want to leave.

I was stubborn though, and David could see how much had changed in me during my time on my own. I was fierce and independent and I'd done amazing things with turning the small-town newspaper into a thriving business that the community loved and cherished. He'd seen me with my cousins, reconnecting after so much sadness. In the end he couldn't take that away from me, and the fact that Lexi had chosen a college in Iowa only helped him realize he didn't care where he lived as long as he was with his favorite girls.

The Monster ran through the house, hearing Lexi's voice, and jumped up at her, assuming her girl would catch her. And as always, she did.

"Oh, my little Monster, I missed you so much!" She smothered her growing pup with kisses and declarations of love.

Matt cleared his throat and Lexi looked to him, eyebrow raised in question.

"I just wanted to make sure you remembered I'm here too, that's all," he said, giving the dog a scratch on the head.

"Oh, was little Matty getting jealous?" she joked, scratching Matt on the head and under his chin. They giggled, and the Monster yipped, happy to be a part of the excitement.

After the tour, I told Lexi not to drop her bags in the guest room.

"You're not staying here," I told her. "This one belongs to your dad and me." I pointed out the back door. "You're out there."

Lexi smiled, her eyes brightening.

"I get Wild Rose House?" she asked, squealing a bit. "But wasn't someone else going to move in?"

I rolled my eyes and threw my hands up.

"Well, you know Ty and Nathaniel are living together in Iowa City," I started. "He just isn't ready to move back; he probably never will. But he visits quite a bit, so we've been able to see him a lot. Lauren refuses to leave her house, even though it's way too big for just her most of the year. Sophie's there with her this summer at least. Whenever we ask about it Lauren talks our ears off about equity and the beauty of having a house paid off. Blah blah, I don't know. Penny won't take another handout from us, and she loves her little apartment downtown, anyway. That leaves this little place empty, so I figured you'd be able to fill it, at least for the summer. What do you think?"

Lexi turned to Matt and asked if he'd help her get her stuff from the Jeep. "Yes, Ma'am," he told her, saluting. The two young adults went off to take care of business, leaving David and me alone in the house again.

"Are you happy?" David asked me, sliding his arms around me. He knew I'd been so nervous about having our daughter back home and wanted everything to go well. He'd had to leave so much for work and was eager to get back to us for good and spend his retirement finding things he enjoyed. Maybe he'd take up farming, he joked once with a smirk. Or quilting with Dottie.

"Yeah, I am," I whispered into his shoulder, leaning in against him. David pulled me close and told me he was happiest when everyone was together.

"This is going to be a beautiful summer," he told me. "Hopefully a little less eventful this year," he added with a wink.

"Well then, it looks like we got our happy ever after," I said, standing on my tiptoes to kiss him lightly. "Now let's go get our Wild

Rose Girl." We stopped at the back door, taking in the backyard and the little house with the growing flowers in front.

So much happiness existed in the air around the house and the field. So much pain too. I held on to David a moment longer, taking it all in. I was ready to claim my happy ever after. For Lexi, for Tina, for myself.

For everyone who'd ever been a part of Wild Rose House.

About the Author

Shannon Ambroson is a neurodivergent Millennial who drinks too much coffee, reads a lot, and always chooses Converse over heels. Wild Rose Girls is her first published novel. Before diving into the world of fiction she worked as a journalist, a freelance writer, and a barista, along with years of volunteer work with military spouse groups. She lives with her husband, teen daughters, dog, and two kittens outside Atlanta.

https://www.shannonambrosonwriter.com